Kaylee's frightened sobs had awakened him.

He'd grabbed his gun from beneath his pillow and bolted upright in one smooth motion, sweeping his gun back and forth, seeking out whatever had scared her. Then she'd thrashed and moaned again, and he'd realized there weren't any bad guys hiding in the shadows of their hotel room. The bad guys were hiding in the shadowed recesses of her mind.

His heart had clenched in his chest at how terrified and pale she looked as the nightmare gripped her. So he'd put his gun away and leaned over, ready to shake her awake. But the moment he'd whispered her name and then placed his hand on her shoulder, she'd stilled, then rolled over to face him with a smile on her face, fast asleep.

He'd pulled his hand back and studied her beautiful face, watching her expression to make sure the nightmare was really gone.

HOSTAGE NEGOTIATION

LENA DIAZ

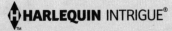
HARLEQUIN INTRIGUE®

Thank you Allison Lyons and Nalini Akolekar.

This book is dedicated to some awesome family members who cheer me on and keep me going—Denise, Estelle, George, Jaime, Jennifer, Isabelle, Laura, Letha, Lisa, Mavis Marie, Michelle and Sean. I love you all.

ISBN-13: 978-0-373-69930-8

Hostage Negotiation

Copyright © 2016 by Lena Diaz

Recycling programs for this product may not exist in your area.

Printed in U.S.A.

www.Harlequin.com

Lena Diaz was born in Kentucky and has also lived in California, Louisiana and Florida, where she now resides with her husband and two children. Before becoming a romantic suspense author, she was a computer programmer. A former Romance Writers of America Golden Heart® Award finalist, she has won a prestigious Daphne du Maurier Award for Excellence in mystery and suspense. To get the latest news about Lena, please visit her website, lenadiaz.com.

Books by Lena Diaz

Harlequin Intrigue

Marshland Justice

Missing in the Glades
Arresting Developments
Deep Cover Detective
Hostage Negotiation

The Marshal's Witness
Explosive Attraction
Undercover Twin
Tennessee Takedown
The Bodyguard

CAST OF CHARACTERS

Zack Scott—The new chief of police in Mystic Glades, Florida. When a killer sets his sights on a beautiful stranger, Zack's first Mystic Glades case may become his last.

Kaylee Brighton—All this young woman wanted was a relaxing vacation. Instead, she was abducted and had to fight for her life. Now she's back, forcing past her fears to help Chief Scott find another missing woman. But the killer has other plans—for Kaylee.

Cole Larson—Collier County Sheriff's Office deputy, Cole is assisting Zack in setting up the new Mystic Glades Police Department.

Mary Watkins—She disappeared in the Everglades and has never been seen again. Was she the victim of the Ghost of Mystic Glades? Or have the Glades become home to a very real killer?

Sandy Gonzalez—Runs Aventuras Travel Agency based out of Miami. She planned and arranged the vacation package for Kaylee. But then Kaylee was abducted. Does Sandy blame Kaylee for the negative impact to her agency?

Rick Carlson—A rookie deputy with the Collier County Sheriff's Office. This is Rick's second career, and he's one of the first to volunteer to help with the search. Is that because he truly wants to help? Or is there another, more sinister, reason for him wanting to be involved?

Jasper Carraway—This Florida Fish and Wildlife Conservation Commission officer is abducted by the same man who abducted Kaylee. Will he escape? Or will he become the killer's next victim?

Chapter One

The campfire crackled and cast eerie light and shadows on its young audience, their faces rapt with attention, eyes big and round as the storyteller wove his tale. Sitting on the opposite side of the fire a few feet away from the children, Mystic Glades Chief of Police Zack Scott and his friend, Collier County Detective Cole Larson, waited for the story to be over so they could escort their young charges back into town.

Just fifty yards away, beneath an alligator-shaped sign on an archway, was the entrance to the eccentric, quirky town of Mystic Glades. Hidden deep in the Florida Everglades, several miles from the section of I-75 known as Alligator Alley, the town was home to a couple hundred residents. Downtown consisted of one long dirt and gravel street with wooden clapboard one- and two-story businesses lining both sides. And in front of the buildings was a wide, wooden boardwalk.

The whole setup screamed "Spaghetti Western," an image that was enhanced by the fact that many residents wore firearms either holstered in plain sight or hidden in their pockets—a dangerous tradition that Zack was determined to change. But so far he wasn't getting much traction, the argument being that the residents needed their guns because the snakes and alligators outnumbered them a hundred to one.

They had a point.

Everything that made Mystic Glades a difficult town, both to live in and police, made it "charming" and "interesting" to tourists. A recently created airboat tour company brought them up through the canals every morning and back home again at night, except for the few who stayed at the equally new bed-and-breakfast.

The town wasn't on any map and was difficult to reach by car. The only reason that Zack knew about it was because his friend Cole had recruited him to become Mystic Glades's first-ever official law-enforcement officer.

But as Zack sat on the rotten log, watching a mosquito buzz in front of his face—the same mosquito he'd been trying to swat away for the past two minutes—he was trying to remember why he'd thought that leaving his job a few months ago as a police officer in Murray, Kentucky, to come here had seemed like a good idea.

Smack! Got the bloodthirsty little sucker. He flicked the squashed mosquito off his arm then realized the clearing had gone silent. He jerked his head up. A dozen young faces stared at him, the storyteller's spell broken. And on the other side of the campfire, gray-haired self-appointed town elder, Buddy Johnson, the man in charge of tonight's entertainment and the owner of the airboat company, narrowed his eyes with disapproval.

Cole gave Zack a shove. "You're in trouble now," he whispered. "Gandalf the Grey is not amused."

Zack shoved him back. "I think I can handle the wrath of a man old enough to be my grandfather."

"Don't underestimate him. It might be the last mistake you ever make." Cole waggled his eyebrows then laughed.

Zack shoved him so hard that Cole fell off the log they were sitting on. Zack smirked at his friend's aggravated look. Cole was probably dying to let loose with a string of curses but couldn't with the kids within hearing distance.

"Sorry, Buddy," Zack called out as he offered a hand to help Cole up. "Didn't mean to interrupt your story."

Buddy shook his head as if he thought Zack was daft. "It's not some made-up *story*. It's the truth." He waved his hands at the trees and soggy marsh of the Everglades surrounding them. "People disappear in these woods and are never heard from again. Mark my words. The Ghost of Mystic Glades is real." He dramatically looked at each of the children until they were all focused on him once again. "And if you don't mind your parents, and do your homework and your chores, he'll come after you one day."

Cole let out a deep sigh. Zack groaned. They both rose to their feet.

Zack could already see the kind of day he'd have tomorrow—an endless parade of concerned parents berating him for giving their kids nightmares. "I think we've had enough for one night. Thank you, Buddy, for…*entertaining* my future deputies."

Cole snickered beside him. Zack would make him pay for that later.

"Let's put out this fire and get back to town," Zack said.

A collective grumble went up from the children.

"But I want to hear more about the Ghost of Mystic Glades," one of the older girls in the group complained.

"Me, too," the boy beside her called out, even though the wide-eyed look on his face said he'd rather go without dessert for a week than hear one more scary thing from Buddy Johnson. Zack figured the kid must have a major crush on the girl who'd spoken or he'd never have pretended his agreement.

Buddy waved his hands again, like a wizard casting spells—or an old man who should have known better than to terrify middle schoolers. "About five months ago, the Ghost of Mystic Glades kidnapped a woman named Sue Ellen Fullerton. She was never heard from again. Three months ago another young woman disappeared after going for a walk down a nature trail in the Everglades just a hop-skip down Alligator Alley from here. Her name was Kaylee Brighton. She just…vanished, without a trace. No one has ever heard from her again either." He waved his arms with a flourish and the kids made "ooooh" noises.

Cole started laughing.

"Enough," Zack called out to Buddy then frowned at his friend. "Help me get them back to town before Buddy tells them the Loch Ness monster is lurking in the swamp. If we don't nip this disaster right now, I just may set the world record for shortest career ever as chief of police."

"Nah." Cole motioned for the children to come over to them for the short trek back into town. "Your job is safe. No one else wants it."

Zack sighed. Cole was teasing, but the words he'd said were true. It had taken several disasters, and a brand-new influx of tourists over the past few years to finally convince the hermit-like but growing town to admit they needed their own police force, instead of relying on Collier County or Broward County Police to step in when things went south. With Mystic Glades set so far back from the interstate, response times from both counties could range from twenty minutes to an hour depending on how far away any available deputies might be.

Even though they'd hired Zack to do the job, he

met with opposition and resentment every day from the majority of the residents. Many preferred their previous lawless existence. The rest of them seemed to consider him a necessary evil and a hindrance. And they went out of their way to remind him that even though his presence was a necessity, that didn't mean they were happy that he was there. They'd expressed their discontent by supergluing the front door shut on the brand-new police station.

And by switching the hot and cold water taps in the station's only bathroom.

And, the prank that had garnered the most laughter and amusement, at his expense—sneaking a black panther into his bedroom while he slept—after taking his weapons out of the room to protect the panther. Never mind protecting *him*. He'd later found out that the panther—affectionately named Sampson—had no teeth and was the semitame pet of the woman who owned The Moon and Star just down the street from the station. But no one had bothered to tell *him* that the panther was harmless. He still flushed with embarrassment when he remembered how fast he'd broken out the bedroom window and hauled butt down the street to escape—key word being *butt*, as in *butt naked*.

"Who plays caboose this time?" Cole asked.

Buddy was already leading their little troop in a single file line back to town, with the girl who'd been interested in hearing more of his stories at the head of the line beside him. From the animated look on the girl's face, Zack could only imagine what kinds of tales Buddy was sharing with her now.

"I'll get the fire. You can be the caboose," Zack said.

"Having you do all the work is fine by me."

Cole waved and hurriedly took his place at the end of the line to make sure that no one ventured off the path. Zack imagined the real reason Cole was so happy to shepherd the kids back to town was because it meant he could go home to his new bride that much sooner. He and Silver owned and lived in Mystic Glades's only B and B.

Zack grabbed the bucket and shovel that he kept stored near the clearing for dousing the weekly campfires. He scooped up some swamp water and poured it on the fire then stirred the embers with the shovel, repeating the process until everything was cool to the touch. By the time he was satisfied that the fire was dead and out, with no potential to flare up later and endanger anyone, the line of children had long ago passed beneath the archway into town.

He stowed the bucket and shovel by an old oak tree for the next story time, optimistically assuming that there would *be* a next time after tonight's scary-story fiasco. Winning over the children was part of his plan to win over their parents and was one of the reasons that he'd started story times and hiking and camping activities with the kids. The sooner he could get the residents to support his role as chief, the sooner he could sleep without one eye open, dreading their next prank.

Of course, if he didn't fill the two open deputy positions, there was no chance of running a viable police force and gaining the respect of the citizens. Hopefully, at least one of the candidates that Cole had helped him line up to interview tomorrow in Naples could be convinced to move to Mystic Glades to take up a position. All of the previous candidates had bolted after reaching the part of the interview where Zack gave them the lowdown on life in his town. He was starting to think he should just lie and trick someone into moving here. After all, that was basically what Cole had done to him.

Cole's wife's inn had only recently been rebuilt after a drug runner, using Mystic Glades as his personal home base, had burned it to the ground. The drug runner had been dealt with—thanks largely to Cole—and the town was a safe place to live once again.

But since Cole worked quite a distance away in Naples, he wanted to make sure the town, and the woman he loved, always had someone nearby to maintain order. So he'd ruthlessly used the town's gratitude toward him to pressure them into putting up the funds to create the Mystic Glades Police Station and everything that entailed. In return, they'd made him promise to bring in someone worthy of the job as chief who could then bring in the staff that he needed to get the job done. That's why Cole had contacted Zack.

They'd met three years ago at a law-enforcement seminar in Nashville and had become fast friends. Cole knew that Zack was a career officer, hungry for advancement. So he'd dangled the carrot of becoming chief of police, of starting his own department from the ground up, betting that Zack would bite. Which he did, resigning his position and moving to Mystic Glades without even having visited the area first.

He should have been furious with Cole for tricking him, for painting the town to be a tropical paradise with a supportive township that would welcome his presence. Nothing could be further from the truth. But he knew how deeply Cole cared for Silver. His love for her had been clear over the phone, and painfully obvious once Zack had seen the two of them together. That was when Zack's anger at his friend's trickery had dissipated. Because Zack knew what it was like to love a woman that way. He'd found his soul mate right out of college. But before they could begin to plan their life together, she'd discovered she had breast cancer.

Four months later she was gone.

Zack closed his eyes, his body going rigid as pain washed through him. It had been five years since he'd lost Jo Lynne, and still the memories hit him when he least expected, making it hard to breathe. Coming here, leaving behind all of the places that constantly reminded him of her, had been even more of an incentive than becoming chief of police. But he was finding that age-old saying to be true—you can't run from your past.

Especially if you carry the scars around inside you.

A high-pitched shriek shattered the night. Zack's eyes flew open, his hand going to the pistol holstered on his hip as he studied the trees and bushes, turning a full three-sixty, trying to figure out where the sound had originated. Everything was quiet and still. Even the crickets. But not for long. They started up again, their rhythmic chirps punctuated by the occasional deep-throated croak of a bullfrog. But that shriek, the sound that had the hairs on the back of his neck standing on end, didn't repeat. And the acoustics in this swampy, tree-filled part of the Glades made it impossible to pinpoint the direction where the sound had come from.

What had he heard? Could it have been a *scream*? As far as he knew, no one else was out here. The town was isolated, nothing around it for miles. And the residents knew better than to roam the swamp at night. There were far too many four-legged critters scavenging for food to make that safe. So what could have made that screech?

A swishing noise had him jerking his head up to see a large brown owl overhead, flapping its wings and gliding into the clearing. It landed on a cypress stump about ten feet away, blinking its dark, round eyes and watching him with lazy curiosity. The tension drained out of him and he let out a shaky laugh. An owl. He'd nearly drawn his gun on a bird. He shook his head and dropped his hand from the butt of his pistol. If his brothers back in Murray, Kentucky, could see him now, they'd laugh their fool heads off.

Having grown up painfully poor in the eastern part of the state, there'd been no video games or cable TV to keep him and his three brothers out of trouble. So they'd chased away boredom by playing cops and robbers in the thick woods and hills, or hide-and-seek in the twelve-foot-high rows of cornstalks on their daddy's farm.

As they'd grown older, they'd learned to track and hunt, doing their part to thin out the herds of deer that would otherwise suffer and die of starvation or disease—or destroy the crops Zack's family depended on to keep their bellies full and a roof over their heads. So he was quite familiar with the kinds of wild animals that roamed that part of the country, from the tracks they left to the sounds they made. But two months in southern Florida was hardly enough for him to get used to the wildlife around here. He'd just have to assume that the screech he'd heard had been made by the owl that was still blinking at him, as if wondering if he'd make a good next meal.

Maybe he'd Google owls later and figure out what

kind this one was. But he'd have to wait until tomorrow morning's planned trip into Naples. He certainly couldn't search the internet here. Mystic Glades was notorious for interfering with the signals of electronic equipment, and he'd long ago given up trying to surf the net on his laptop. Even the GPS in his pickup truck rarely worked out here. Which was another reason that prospective deputies weren't keen on moving to the Glades.

Living life without internet was inconceivable to many, downright prehistoric to others. He was still in withdrawal himself. Snapping a picture of some crazy thing he'd come across in the swamp and texting it to his buddies back home or his family was so second nature that he still found himself pulling out his phone several times a week to do just that.

Until he remembered he was living in the land that time forgot.

He started down the path again, but he kept a close eye on his surroundings. While residents of this backwater town, including the children, understood the dangers and took them in stride, this was all new to him. He was still learning how to acclimate himself to the hostile environment so he didn't become a gator snack or experience the painful, possibly poisonous bite of a snake. Cottonmouths and rattlers weren't uncommon out here.

But it wasn't reptiles or the slithering inhabitants

of the Everglades that had him studying everything with a keener eye than usual.

Buddy's outlandish stories about monsters and people disappearing in the swamp had obviously gotten to him just as it had the children. Because even though he knew that mournful, terrified-sounding screech had to have come from the owl, he couldn't help a niggling doubt that kept running through his mind.

What if I'm wrong?

Chapter Two

Tears streamed from her burning eyes. Blinking furiously, she stumbled to a halt and braced herself against a tree, her stiff fingers curling against the rough bark. Her breaths came in quick, shallow gasps as she raised a hand to block out the bright morning sunlight streaking down through the canopy of tree branches overhead.

How many times had she prayed for sunlight, to feel its warmth on her skin? To breathe in air that was fresh and clean, not musty and heavy with her own stink? She'd whispered that prayer hundreds of times. But not today. Today the light was a curse, a harsh, blinding torch to eyes used to utter darkness; an enemy in her desperate bid for freedom.

Swiping at the tears, she took off again, leaping over a branch in her path. Then she put on a fresh burst of speed, grimacing each time her bare feet hit a rock or sharp twig. A knobby cypress root seemed to jump up from out of nowhere, tripping her. She landed hard on all fours.

A burst of fiery pain shot through her knees and she bit her lip to keep from crying out. The metallic taste of blood filled her mouth and she pounded her fist on the ground in frustration. Pain lanced through her body, from the stinging cuts on her feet to the throbbing in her head that never seemed to go away.

You're wasting time. Hurry! You have to be miles away before he realizes you're gone.

She staggered to her feet, risking a quick look over her shoulder.

What if he'd already discovered that she'd escaped? What if he was tracking her, right now?

He won't find me. I'll be okay. He'll give up the search.

A bitter laugh welled up inside her. No. He would never give up. He would keep looking, searching, hunting. He was fast. And cunning. And more terrifying than any nightmare she'd ever had.

A thud sounded behind her.

No! It can't be him.

But what if it is?

She surged forward on wobbly legs, pouring what little strength she had left into trying to run. Tired. She was so tired. And hungry. And thirsty. All she wanted to do was curl up in a ball and surrender to exhaustion.

Don't give up! He nearly killed you when you ran the first time. If he catches you again, he will *kill you, but only after he punishes you.*

A sob rose in her throat at the thought of enduring another one of his "punishments."

Thud. Thud. Thud.

Footsteps! *Oh, God. No. Please.* She stumbled, caught herself against a tree. Fell. Pushed herself up. Started running again.

She couldn't deny the truth any longer. He was following her. She knew it even without seeing him, by the way her joints tightened with fear, the way her heart slammed against her ribs so hard she thought they'd crack. The very air around her seemed charged with menace, a black, choking fog of evil.

More thumps. Faster. He was running. He must have found her tracks. He was *so* close. A whimper escaped between her clenched teeth.

I don't want to die. Twenty-three years isn't enough. I want a family, babies. How can I die when I haven't even lived?

Another sound interrupted the quiet of the Glades. A low rumble. Wait. Was that a car? Leaves crackled and twigs snapped somewhere up ahead, as if they were being crunched beneath tires. Yes! Someone was driving a car through the woods. Had she finally found civilization? Was there a road through this horrible, cursed, endless swamp? *Hurry, hurry.* She couldn't let them pass her by. This might be her only chance.

She ran full out. She didn't even try to be quiet anymore.

Neither did he.

A roar of rage erupted behind her. She whimpered again and hated herself for it.

Don't look. Don't turn around.

The car was coming up fast. Would she make it? This time she couldn't stop herself from looking over her shoulder, to see how close *he* was. A choked sob escaped her. She saw the leather mask he wore through a break in the trees, the gaping hole over his mouth.

He smiled.

She choked on a sob of terror. A horn blared. She whirled around. The grill of a dark vehicle filled her line of vision. She screamed as it slammed into her, tossing her through the air. The boggy ground rushed up to meet her. Excruciating pain slammed through the side of her head, her hip, as she flopped end over end to land on her stomach in a tangle of arms and legs. She lay unmoving, her cheek pressed against the ground, her gaze fastened on the bushes and trees fifteen feet away.

A door slammed. Running footsteps came toward her from the direction of the vehicle. And at the edge of the tree line, directly across from her, *he* stopped. Watching her. His feral smile vicious and deadly, promising retribution.

She let out a small cry.

"Miss. Can you hear me?" A man's deep voice, thick with concern as he knelt beside her, his back turned to evil incarnate.

The devil slowly drew a large, serrated knife from the holder strapped to his thigh.

She sucked in a breath and tried to warn the stranger. But she couldn't make her lips form any words. Blood bubbled up in her throat, choking her. *Can't breathe. Can't. Breathe.*

The stranger kneeling beside her, ever so carefully, tilted her head. Her airway cleared. She coughed and tried again to warn him.

Run! She tried to tell him. *He'll kill you!* She tried to raise her hand, to wave toward the devil. But she didn't seem to have control over her body anymore. Everything was going numb. And cold, so cold.

Satan took a step toward the stranger, knife raised.

"My name is Zack Scott." Her would-be rescuer leaned down into her field of vision, his handsome face lined with worry. He scooted a bunched-up cloth of some kind beneath her head. "I'm the chief of police of Mystic Glades. Just hold on. I've got you."

The devil paused.

"Turn around." She forced the words past her bruised lips, but they came out a gurgle.

"Don't try to talk. Lie as still as you can. Don't move."

A rumbling noise echoed through the trees. Another car? Brakes squealed. A door slammed. Footsteps pounded.

The devil jerked back beside a tree, a shadow amongst shadows.

"What the…?" Another man's voice. Dirt sliding as he dropped to his knees beside Zack. "What happened? Who is she?"

"She ran out in front of my truck. Try your phone, Cole. We might be far enough from Mystic Glades to have cell service."

Turn around, Zack. Look behind you, Cole. Her fingers curled helplessly into the dirt as she stared at Satan. Why couldn't she make herself form the words to warn them? Her throat was so tight. Everything hurt.

Zack's warm fingers pressed against her neck. "Her pulse is weak." He glanced toward Cole then nodded and looked at her again. "The call went through. Help is on the way. You're going to be okay. Everything's going to be okay. Just, please, hold on."

The devil's eyes flashed.

She whimpered and surrendered to the darkness.

Chapter Three

Zack paced the hospital waiting room.

"Will you stop already?" Cole shifted in his chair. "You're making everyone around us dizzy. And you're making *me* want to slug you. Sit down."

Zack was surprised to realize that most of the dozen or so people scattered around the large waiting room were indeed watching him. He rubbed the back of his neck and made himself sit beside Cole. But keeping still proved impossible. Nervous energy had his foot tapping up and down as he leaned forward, resting his forearms on the tops of his thighs.

After a few minutes of sitting, he jumped to his feet again.

Cole let out a low curse.

"The ambulance brought our Jane Doe here over two hours ago," Zack complained. "Someone should have told us something by now. What if she's…what if she's dead? What if she's alive but paralyzed? I tilted her head when she was lying on the road, shoved one of my socks under her neck to keep her face angled up. What if she had a spinal cord injury and I made it worse?"

"Is that why you're acting like a caged tiger? You blame yourself?"

"Well, of course I blame myself. I ran her over with my truck. Who else should I blame?"

"*Her.* She ran out in front of you. And you didn't run her over. You tapped her with the bumper."

"Tapped?" Zack gave his friend an incredulous look. "She went somersaulting through the air like a rag doll and…" He fisted his hands, trying to block out the memory of her body flipping end over end, landing in a crumpled heap. That she'd still been breathing when he'd reached her was a miracle. But then, when blood had bubbled from her mouth, he'd… "I shouldn't have moved her head."

"She was choking on her own blood according to what you told the EMTs when they arrived. The reason you propped her head up was so she could breathe. Or am I wrong about that?"

"No. But I—"

"But *nothing*. You did what you had to do to save her life. So jump off the guilt-trip train already. Instead, ask yourself what she was even doing there in the first place. You saw her clothes—dirty, torn, not just from the accident either, is my guess. And she wasn't even wearing shoes."

"Yeah, I know. Her hair was matted, really matted. And her skin was grimy, as if she'd been out there a long time. There's something really wrong here. But I can't even begin to focus on starting an investigation until I know whether she's going to be okay."

And, God, please, with no life-altering deficits caused by him.

"Since you're still setting up the police department in Mystic Glades, my boss has already sent men out to the swamp to start checking things out. And he's fine with me staying here as long as needed, until we get some answers. And an update on our Jane Doe."

Zack nodded his thanks.

On the other side of the waiting room there was a short hallway that led into the bowels of the emergency room. Doctors and nurses kept going in and out of the door at the end, but so far none of them had spoken to either him or Cole.

"Why hasn't anyone come out to talk to us?"

Instead of answering, Cole crossed his arms, obviously giving up on trying to talk Zack out of worrying.

The door to the ER opened again. And just like dozens of times before, a nurse stepped out. But this one didn't hurry away. Instead, she stopped at the information desk and spoke to the volunteer sitting there. Zack watched them intently. The volunteer checked her clipboard then pointed toward Zack and Cole. *Finally.*

As the nurse hurried toward them, Cole rose to stand shoulder to shoulder with Zack.

"Just remember—" Cole kept his voice low "—no matter what she tells us, none of this is your fault."

Maybe. Maybe not. But nothing could change the fact that it was his truck that had slammed into the young woman who was fighting for her life right now, assuming that she was even still alive. If he'd killed her…no, he wouldn't go there, *couldn't* go there. Having something like that on his conscience was a burden he didn't think he could bear. She *had* to make it.

"Chief Scott, Detective Larson?" She looked from one to the other, her brows arched in question.

"I'm Chief Scott," Zack clarified. "And this is Detective Larson."

"Ma'am." Cole nodded.

"I'm Miss Murphy, one of the ER nurses. Doctor Varley is attending to your Jane Doe and wanted me to give you an update."

"Then she's…she isn't…" Zack stopped, not wanting to voice his fears out loud, afraid he'd jinx the outcome.

She gave him a sympathetic smile. "She's alive, if that's what you're asking. And she's doing very well, all things considered."

He let out a ragged breath. Then her words sank in. "All things considered? What does that mean? Is she paralyzed? Is she—"

"No, no, goodness, no. She's not paralyzed. Her prognosis is very good, actually. I take it from your response that you're the one who hit her?"

He winced. "Yes, ma'am."

She patted his forearm. "Rest assured. A slight concussion, bruises and a minor tear in the soft tissues of her throat are all that you can take credit for. Most everything else is inconsistent with being hit by a car."

Zack exchanged a confused look with Cole. "Everything else?"

It was her turn to look confused. "Well, yes. The burns, the dehydration, cuts, abrasions."

"Burns?" they asked at the same time.

"Dehydration?" Zack added.

Her brows drew down. "You didn't know?"

"Know *what*?" Zack asked. "Did she burn herself in a campfire then go looking for help and got lost? Is that why she was dehydrated?"

She looked around then stepped closer as if to make sure that no one else could hear her. "Your Jane Doe has extensive bruising all over her body. Judging by their coloration, many of the bruises are days, or even weeks, old. She's malnourished, and chunks of her hair look as if they've been pulled out by the roots. The burns that I mentioned? No campfire would cause the circular patterns on her abdomen and back. If I had to guess, I'd say they're cigarette burns."

From the expression on his friend's face, Cole was just as shocked as Zack was. And just as angry.

"Like I said, the concussion and esophageal tear," she continued, without giving either of them a chance to ask her any questions, "can be attributed to being hit by a vehicle. But the other injuries don't appear to be from an accident." She cleared her throat, looking uncomfortable.

Other injuries. Did she mean more than what she'd already mentioned?

"Miss Murphy," Zack said, "you called her Jane Doe. Didn't she tell you her name?"

She shook her head. "No. She hasn't spoken. She was unconscious when she arrived and woke up inside the CT scanner, confused and combative. We had to sedate her for her own safety. The doctor should be finished stitching her up soon. Then we'll admit her, take her upstairs to a private room, where she can sleep off the effects of the sedative. I'd say that you can ask her questions then, but as exhausted and frail as she is, she'll probably sleep for hours. Maybe even until late tomorrow."

The idea of waiting that long to question the woman certainly wasn't welcome. But right now Zack was more concerned with discovering the details that the nurse seemed to be holding back.

"The *other injuries* that you mentioned, can you be more specific?"

She hesitated, biting her lower lip in indecision.

"Ma'am," Cole spoke up. "We're both law-enforcement officers, and that young woman is currently our responsibility. If we're going to find the person who hurt her, we need to know exactly what happened."

She leaned in toward them. "The bruising I mentioned...there were dark, chafed circles on her wrists and ankles. Doctor Varley believes she was restrained, for an extended period of time."

Zack grew very still. "Someone tied her up?"

"We think so, yes. And the X-rays showed some hairline fractures in her forearms, basically healed now, but still recent. I'm sure you're aware that breaks like that are characteristic of someone raising their arms to—"

"Defend themselves," Zack finished for her.

She nodded. "Now, if you'll excuse me, I have to get back to my patient." She took off across the room before either of them could stop her and disappeared through a swinging door marked Authorized Personnel Only.

"What's going on?" Zack kept his voice low, aware that many eyes were watching them. "She was, what, someone's *prisoner*? Long enough for fractures to heal?"

"Maybe the Ghost of Mystic Glades isn't a myth, after all," Cole said. At Zack's aggravated look, he held up his hands in surrender. "I know, I know. But, inappropriate or not, you were thinking it, too."

He was right. Zack *had* been thinking that, and remembering what else Buddy Johnson had said at last night's ill-fated campfire story hour. Buddy had said that two women had gone missing in the swamp. What were their names? Sue Ellen something, and

Kaylee Brighton? Was it possible that Jane Doe was one of those women?

Where before Zack had assumed that Buddy had made up his claims to add flavor to his story, now he wasn't sure. He'd have to check the sheriff's records in Naples to see if any missing persons reports had been filed.

Obviously, no ghost had done those terrible things to the woman they'd found. But Zack didn't want to believe that someone was abducting women and using the Glades to hide their crimes.

Cole's phone buzzed in his pocket and he pulled it out, frowning at the screen. "Give me a minute." He stepped away to take the call, covering his other ear to drown out the sounds of the busy hospital around them.

Zack curled his fingers into fists at his sides. The young woman, their Jane Doe, whom he guessed to be in her mid-twenties, had possibly been abducted and held prisoner. She'd been hurt, abused and yet, she'd been running through the woods just a few miles from Mystic Glades. Why? Was her abductor playing games, letting his victim run while he hunted her like prey? Or had she managed to escape when she'd stumbled out onto the road?

It seemed hard to believe that she could have been out in the swamp for very long, at least not that close to the town where he lived, without being discovered. Yes, the area was sparsely populated. But residents and even the occasional Everglades tourist were known for hiking and canoeing through the beautiful woods and canals nearby, at least when the sun was out and they could keep a careful eye out for dangerous animals and reptiles. Surely, someone would have heard her cry for help if she'd been out there long enough to become malnourished and dehydrated. Or had her abductor kept her gagged the whole time so she couldn't scream?

Scream. Oh, God, no. His mouth went dry. He'd heard a shriek last night when he'd been putting out the campfire. And he'd convinced himself it was the owl that had flown into the clearing. Had he actually heard Jane Doe, crying for help, and he'd turned his back on her, leaving her at the mercy of a brutal attacker? The possibility had bile rising in his throat.

Cole frowned as he ended the call and stepped back to him. "You okay? You look a bit green around the gills."

No, he was not okay.

"What was the call about?" he forced past his tight throat. "Obviously not good because you look green, too."

Cole nodded, not denying it. "Those pictures I took in the back of the ambulance did their job. My boss, Lieutenant Drew Shlafer, said the sheriff in Broward County recognized our girl. They're on the way to show the pictures to her family for confirmation, in

Miami." His eyes flashed with anger. "Want to guess how long ago her family reported her missing?"

Zack swallowed the cold, hard knot in his throat, remembering what Buddy had said last night about the Ghost of Mystic Glades and the two women who'd gone missing. "Five months or three months?"

"Three."

Zack swore and vowed to take anything that Buddy Johnson said in the future far more seriously. He probably should interview Buddy to see what else the old man knew.

"Kaylee Brighton?" Zack asked, even though he already knew the answer.

"Bingo."

Zack straightened his shoulders, as if he could brace himself against the terrible burden that now rested squarely in his jurisdiction. "All right. Let's do this by the book and catch this sicko before he hurts anyone else. The Mystic Glades Police Department is officially requesting assistance from the Collier County Sheriff's Office. There won't be any turf wars over this. I'm a one-man operation right now and I need help."

Cole pulled his phone out again. "You got it. I'll talk to Lieutenant Shlafer. I'm sure he'll authorize whatever you need. Maybe we can get some canine trackers out there, too. Figure out where Kaylee was being held and find the lowlife who took her."

"Thanks. I'll touch base with some of my FBI contacts, see if they've got any other missing-persons reports or homicides where the women were abducted and tortured in remote outdoor areas for an extended period of time. But first, I have to talk to Doctor Varley."

"Why?" Cole asked, holding one of his hands over his phone.

As the nurse had done earlier, Zack glanced around the waiting room to make sure that no one was close enough to hear him before he answered. "This has changed from an accident to a felony kidnapping and possible sexual-assault investigation. I want to see whether the doctor can wake up Kaylee and obtain consent to perform a forensic exam. We need to collect any DNA from under her nails, swab and bag her clothes." His jaw tightened. "We need a rape kit."

Chapter Four

Mumbling voices. Whispered conversations. Antiseptic smell. Above her, a muffled, static-filled announcement over an intercom—code blue to room three twenty-eight. Hospital. She was in a hospital. She curled her hands in the sheets and opened her eyes then blinked against the bright, fluorescent lights. Footsteps sounded to her right and the harsh lights switched off, leaving the room dimly lit. Relieved, she blinked and took her first good look around.

And immediately wished she hadn't.

Her room, though large by most hospital standards, was positively claustrophobic since there were five men and a woman crammed inside, all wearing business suits and standing by her bed. Dark pieces of memories swirled through her mind, of being caught, trapped. She recoiled against her pillow and pulled the sheet up to her neck, fighting the panic that was threatening to overwhelm her.

"Back up," a deep voice ordered from her right. "You're scaring her."

Unhappy grumblings filled the room, but "the suits" dutifully stepped away from the bed. She turned her head on her pillow to see who'd spoken, a seventh person, a man whom she hadn't noticed before. Which, now that she saw him, seemed ludicrous. He wasn't the kind of man to fade into the background. There was a certain…intensity about him, an aura of confidence, authority, that commanded attention.

He wasn't unusually tall, standing at about six feet. He had short, light brown hair and dark eyes—hard to tell the exact color from this distance. Trim-waisted, he wore a long-sleeved, button-down blue shirt tucked into khaki pants with a sharp crease that could have sliced butter. His arms were crossed, emphasizing his large biceps and muscular chest. He was obviously fit, powerful, strong—qualities that she should have admired. But for some reason, seeing him made her tense and flooded her with an overwhelming desire to run, escape.

She frowned. Escape? What an odd thought to pop into her head.

"Do you know where you are?"

His voice was gentle, soothing, oddly familiar. The panic that had started inside her at seeing how strong, how powerful he was, began to fade. She'd heard that voice before, somewhere. And it made her feel…safe.

She frowned again. Why would she crave safety? Was she in danger? None of this made sense.

The man with the intense, dark eyes didn't approach her bed. Instead, he stayed by the window, as if he sensed her hesitancy, her confusion, her…fear?

"Hospital," she answered his question. "I'm in a hospital. Not sure which one."

"Naples Community. I'm Chief Zack Scott from Mystic Glades. We…met…earlier. Do you remember?"

He'd winced when he said they'd met. Why? Wait. Naples? Why was she in Naples? That wasn't right. She should have been…where? She tried to think, to remember…anything…but her thoughts were a jumble of blurred images that didn't make sense.

This man, the one in khaki pants…he'd been kneeling over her. When? Why? His face had been lined with concern, his voice gentle as he smoothed her hair out of her eyes.

"Do you know your name?" he asked quietly, from his position by the window.

"Of course I know my name. It's…it's…" She blinked, her breaths coming faster, her pulse slamming in her veins. Why couldn't she remember? Her head throbbed. Her body flushed hot and cold. She raised her hand to her forehead and saw the IV tubing twisted around her arm, tape on the top of her wrist. Ugly purple bruises and lighter yellow ones dotted both of her arms. White bandages were…everywhere. What was going on? She jerked her head up and met the kind eyes of…what did he say his name was? Zack? "I don't… I can't…" She pressed her lips together and shook her head in frustration. "I can't remember."

"It's okay," he assured her. "The doctor said that might happen, because of your concussion, and that any memory loss is most likely temporary. You were in an accident, but you're going to be…fine."

His jaw tightened briefly, as if his choice of words disturbed him. But then he smiled again. "No broken bones. Mostly cuts, scrapes, bruises." He waved his hand toward the others. "Everyone in this room is law enforcement. We're here to talk to you about what happened. There's nothing to be afraid of."

She let his soothing voice wrap around her like a warm blanket, forcing back the panic that threatened to overwhelm her. He'd said she'd been in an accident and that she had a concussion, which made sense since her head was throbbing. It would all come back to her. With this many law-enforcement officers in her room, whatever had happened must have been horrible.

She froze. Wait. Six, no, seven officials standing in her room. Would they do that for an accident victim? Or had the accident been *her* fault? Oh, God. Had she killed someone? Her gaze flew to Zack's. "You said I was in an accident. What happened?" she asked. "Did I…did I hurt someone?"

"No, no, of course not. You didn't hurt anyone." He took a step toward her.

She tensed, pushing back against her pillow.

He immediately stopped and shot a glance at a dark-haired man in a gray suit standing on the left side of her bed. "Maybe we should get her doctor, Cole. We're upsetting her. This is too much, too fast. She's not ready."

Another man, at the foot of her bed, braced his hands on the metal railing. "We can't wait, Chief Scott. For all we know, the man who abducted her is after another woman right now. Or he could be holding the other missing woman. We need answers."

"Abducted?" The word rasped past her dry lips. "I was abducted? You said there was an accident. I don't understand."

The kind man, Zack, narrowed his eyes at the one who'd just spoken before looking at her. "You don't remember what happened? The woods? The marsh?"

She shook her head. Wait. No. *No, no, no.* She squeezed her eyes shut. The devil's face swam in her vision, wide slits in the mask revealing dark, dead eyes. Except when he was hurting her. Then those eyes shined with an unholy light. She remembered something sharp, no, something hot, burning her back. Chains, ropes, her arms tied above her head. A box. Dark. Musty. The choking feel of him pressing her down, down. Oh, God. She covered her face with her hands.

"You're safe," that deep, soothing voice whispered again, closer now. Not the devil's voice. Zack's voice. *The man who'd saved her.*

"No one can hurt you here. You're safe. You're safe," he whispered, over and over, as if he knew what she needed to hear in order to fight off the panic threatening to choke her.

"Chief." Even without looking, Kaylee recognized the impatience in the man's voice as he spoke again from the foot of the bed. "I need to ask her questions. We don't have time for—"

"Make time," her protector snapped. She heard him step closer to the bed. And this time it didn't scare her. "You're in a hospital," he told her again. "You're going to be okay. There's nothing to worry about. We'll all leave and give you time to—"

"Chief Scott, that's not—"

"We'll leave," he repeated, cutting off the suit's complaint, his voice firm. "We'll come back and talk when she's ready, not a moment before."

She shook her head and forced herself to pull her hands down from over her eyes. She didn't want to be alone. Not again. When she was alone, he always found her—when she was awake, when she was asleep, in her nightmares. She looked at each of the people circling the bed. Strangers. All of them. She turned her head. But this man, the one on her right, the one with concern stamped in his expression, didn't feel like a stranger—in spite of the power coiled inside those muscles, power that should have terrified her. Instead, he made her feel protected. Safe.

And she hadn't felt safe in a very long time.

She clutched the bed railing. "Make them go. Make them go away... Zack...*please*."

Something flickered in his eyes. Surprise?

He gave her a tight nod. "We'll go. I'll get the doctor." He motioned to the others. The room began to empty and he started to follow everyone out. But as he passed her bed, she reached for him, her fingers clutching at his shirtsleeve. "Wait."

He exchanged a startled look with the one other man left in the room, the one who'd been standing on her left. He now stood in the doorway, holding the door open.

"Yes?" Zack asked, his voice gentle, as soothing as she remembered when he'd knelt beside her on the road.

Just hold on. I've got you.

She tightened her hold on his shirt, half lifting off her pillow. Shame over her cowardice and fear made her face heat with embarrassment, but she still didn't let him go. *Couldn't* let him go. Panic welled inside her, making her feel as if she was about to jump out of her skin.

"Please, stay. I'm..." *Scared. More terrified of being shut in a room with a stranger than of being alone with my thoughts, my nightmares.* "Please." She searched his eyes, blue she realized. Kind eyes. Nothing at all like the cold, dark eyes of her captor. "Don't leave me. Keep me safe."

Understanding dawned in his expression. He gently peeled her fingers from his sleeve and took her hand in his. But instead of closing his fingers around hers, he kept his hand beneath hers, palm up, so that she was holding his hand, not the other way around. He'd obviously done that to keep her from feeling trapped, as if she was in control. It was a small gesture, but it warmed her all the way to her soul.

"I'll stay as long as you want me to," he assured her.

Her breath shuddered out of her on a ragged sigh. "Thank you."

He lightly squeezed her hand in answer then glanced at the man still holding the door open. "Get her doctor, Cole."

Cole nodded and headed into the hallway.

"My name is Kaylee," she said, when he looked at her again. "Kaylee Brighton. I live in Miami."

"I know. We've contacted your parents. They arrived yesterday and sat with you all night. They only went back to their hotel a few hours ago to catch up on some sleep. Now that you've woken up, I'm sure they'll be back here soon."

Joy filled her at his words. There had been times, many times, when she'd despaired of ever seeing her mother and father again. But then she frowned, thinking about what he'd said.

"They sat with me all night?"

He nodded.

"How long…how long have I been here?"

His look turned guarded.

"I'm okay," she assured him. "Don't worry about upsetting me. How long?"

"Cole, Collier County Detective Cole Larson, rode with me in the back of the ambulance that brought you here. That was yesterday morning. Except for a few minutes during the CT scan, you've been unconscious since then. You were sedated, to keep you still while they treated you. The doctor evaluated you again a little while ago and told us he thought that you'd be waking up soon. That's why we were all in your room, so we could talk to you."

He checked the watch on his left wrist, a surprising thing to wear for someone his age—probably late twenties, early thirties. But maybe it was something that came in handy in his line of work—quicker to check a watch than to pull out a cell phone to see what time it was. Funny thing was, she liked to wear watches, too, even though she was younger than him. Go figure. But her own watch was gone. *He'd* taken it. The devil. She shuddered.

"It's six in the evening now," he told her.

"You said I was brought here in an ambulance. I don't remember an ambulance."

"You fainted. You were unconscious."

"*You* called for help."

"No. Cole did."

"But you told him to. I heard you." She tightened her fingers on his. "You saved me." Her throat tightened with unshed tears. "Thank you."

His hand jerked beneath hers and his eyes clouded. "Don't thank me. I hit you with my truck. I very nearly killed you."

She tugged his hand closer, forcing him to lean down. Then she lifted her other hand and gently cupped his face, watching his eyes widen with surprise.

"Zack, if you hadn't hit me with that truck, I'd be dead. You *saved* me. Thank you." Her teeth began to chatter as the dark memories swirled through her mind. "I just wish you could have done it sooner."

The dam burst. Tears streamed unchecked down her face. Deep, gasping sobs racked her body and she turned her face into her pillow and closed her eyes again, anchoring his hand in both of hers, unable to let him go. He was her lifeline, and without him, she feared she would drown.

His other hand stroked her hair back from her face. "Shhh, it's okay. It's okay, Kaylee. You're safe. No one is going to hurt you again. I promise."

A door opened and closed. Footsteps echoed. Whispers floated around her. A beep sounded but it seemed so far away. Dark images bombarded her.

Sharp pain. Burning. Cutting. Her wrists throbbed. Her feet ached. He'd taken her shoes the day he'd taken her. To keep her from running.

Muffled voices filled the room. Zack's voice. Cole's. And…someone else.

She let Zack's hand go and put both her hands over her ears to block out the noise so she could concentrate. There was something she needed to remember. Something niggling at the edge of her consciousness. Something important. What was it?

Another beep.

The door to her box was flung open. The stifling heat escaped and she took a deep breath, filling her lungs with the welcome smell of outdoors. But instead of pulling her out, the devil shoved something inside the box with her and slammed the door. Something warm, and furry. It scrabbled past her, running over her bare feet.

She screamed, kicking at it. She beat her fists against the Plexiglas door, over and over, screaming until her throat was raw.

Voices again in the hospital room. His voice, the kind man, Zack. Her protector. He'd saved her.

She was in the box again, a few days later. Or was it weeks? Blindfolded, which made no sense since it was dark outside. He'd pulled her out and left her standing there, trembling, waiting to see what he would do. Then he'd put her back in the box, closed the doors. She tensed, wondering what creature, what horror to expect this time. And then she heard it, shuffling toward her—a whimper.

That was what she'd needed to remember!

Another beep. Lethargy flooded her veins, dragging her down. They were drugging her. No, she couldn't sleep! She had to tell them what she'd remembered!

With a Herculean effort, she forced her heavy lids open. A man in a white coat was pulling a needle out of her IV tubing. He stood beside the man she now knew was Cole. She jerked to her right. Zack. He was still there, standing by the railing, watching her, his brows drawn down in a look of concern.

She flailed blindly, reaching for him.

His large, warm hand, open-palmed, lifted hers. "It's okay, Kaylee. I promise I won't leave. Rest—"

"Have to tell…" Her tongue felt thick in her mouth. "Have to…tell." She shook her head, trying to clear the dark fog closing over her eyes. Desperately trying to hold on to the memory that she'd fought so hard to retrieve.

"It's just a sedative, to help you rest. Don't fight it," he said. "Go to sleep. I promise I'll watch over you. No one will hurt you. Sleep."

Her eyes fluttered shut against her will. Tears leaked out from the corners. "You have to find her. You have to…save her. He has her, too. Find M…Mary."

ZACK'S EYES WIDENED as he stared down at Kaylee, now lying unconscious on the hospital bed. He jerked his head up and saw the same shocked look on Cole's face that he imagined was on his own.

"Doctor, can you reverse the drugs? Wake her up," Zack demanded.

The doctor's mouth tightened into a hard line. "I could. But I won't. Did you see her pulse reading on the screen before I put her under? Way too fast. She's going to suffer a breakdown, or stroke out, if she's pushed too fast. She's exhausted. Her body needs rest, Chief. And time for her potassium and electrolytes to get back into balance. Don't plan on asking her any more questions for at least twelve hours, probably longer."

Zack swore and carefully freed his hand from Kaylee's before running past Cole and the startled doctor. He yanked the door open and Special Agent Willow, the FBI agent who'd stood at the foot of Kaylee's bed earlier, turned around, stopping midsentence in his conversation with the other officers waiting in the hallway.

"What are the names of the women who are still missing?" Zack demanded, as Cole joined him in the doorway.

"What?" Willow's brow furrowed in confusion.

"You told us earlier that two women besides Kaylee are missing. One of them disappeared five months ago, the other three weeks. You also mentioned that you think they could have been taken by the same man who took Kaylee. What are the women's names?"

"Fullerton and Watkins."

Zack waved his hand impatiently. "Their *first* names. What are their first names?"

"Sue Ellen Fullerton."

"And?"

"Mary. Mary Watkins."

Chapter Five

Zack leaned back against the brick wall of the hospital's outdoor atrium, thankful the recent rains had cleared up, at least momentarily. This quiet enclosed garden, with the sun peeking through the clouds and shining down, might be just what Kaylee Brighton needed.

Over the past few days, she'd been grilled with questions inside her hospital room. But no one could call any of those interviews successful. Hopefully, today's session would finally yield the answers everyone wanted and she could be left in peace.

A nurse sat at a table a few feet away from Kaylee's wheelchair. The psychologist that had been assigned as her advocate crouched down, whispering to her patient. It was the psychologist who'd recommended the change in venue when Kaylee had become agitated and panicked answering questions in her room.

It didn't take a genius to understand why.

The dark bruises and calluses around her wrists and ankles told the story of her being bound for most of the time that she'd been missing. That hospital room probably felt claustrophobic and brought back memories she was trying hard to forget.

Memories they kept asking her to relive.

He hated the necessity of it, of asking a victim to face the most horrible things that had ever happened to them, to dredge up the pain and victimize them all over again. But if he and the other officers were going to find the two missing women, they needed to get as much information as they could from Kaylee. So far, they were batting zero in their search to find the man who'd hurt her, or the woman she'd remembered seeing—Mary Watkins.

In spite of combing the swamp with bloodhounds and search-and-rescue teams, they hadn't even been able to locate where Kaylee had been held. The heavy rains that had rolled in had obliterated footprints, scents, and flooded out much of the area near the road where Zack had found her, making it impassable. Aerial searches in that thickly treed area had proven just as useless. And now that four full days had passed since she'd managed to escape her captor, he wasn't so sure that it was worth putting her through this turmoil anymore. The man who'd held her had to have moved on by now. He could even be in another state. There was no way of knowing.

As Zack watched Special Agent Willow begin questioning Kaylee again, he had to force himself to stay where he was. The therapist felt that Kaylee was too dependent on Zack. Every time he left her room she'd begin to panic and wouldn't calm down until she could see his face. She apparently associated him with safety, because she thought of him as the one who'd saved her from her ordeal. But he couldn't do his job if he had to stay with her the whole time. And she couldn't grow stronger mentally if she kept using him as her security blanket.

Still, keeping his distance was killing him, especially because of how pale she looked, and the hesitant, hurt look in her eyes every time she glanced at him, obviously wondering why he was standing so far away.

If her parents were here twenty-four-seven to support her, maybe she'd be doing better. But while Kaylee was twenty-three, her parents had to both be in their mid-sixties, or maybe even seventies. They appeared to be quite frail, and Kaylee seemed more concerned about them than about herself. From what Zack had gleaned from overhearing the nurses talking, Kaylee would only allow her parents one short visit each day. After that, they grudgingly returned to their hotel room until time to visit again.

Her excuse to them was that she was exhausted and needed time to sleep and recover. While that might be only a slight exaggeration, the rest of what she'd told them was a deliberate lie—that the man who'd taken her had done nothing worse than tie her up and scare her.

She'd explained away the bandages on her arms and legs by saying that she'd cut herself running through the woods to get away. And since her hospital gown covered the rest of her body, she didn't have to explain her other injuries. Even her doctors and nurses couldn't contradict what she'd told her parents, because Kaylee was an adult. Doctor-patient confidentiality kept her secrets safe.

From Zack's viewpoint, Kaylee's parents should have fought harder to stay here with her. She was alone far too much. She needed a support system. Because, while he didn't know what all had happened to her yet, he did know it was a heck of a lot more than just being tied up. He'd seen the pictures the police photographer took of her in the emergency room. He'd seen the bruises, the cuts, the burns.

Kaylee Brighton had endured unspeakable horrors.

Watching her blanch at one of Willow's questions had Zack clamping his jaw so tight that his teeth ached. And when she shot him another one of her haunted looks, silently begging him to come over, this time he was helpless to say no.

Shoving away from the wall, he threaded his way through the patio tables and chairs, not stopping until he reached her side. Daring the detectives to say anything, he crossed his arms and prepared to stop this inquisition if it got out of hand. The relief on Kaylee's face told him he was doing the right thing.

Cole, however, obviously disagreed. He gave Zack

a disapproving frown from his seat beside his boss, Lieutenant Shlafer, who was sitting beside Special Agent Willow. Four other Collier County and Broward County detectives sat behind them in a semicircle.

Paying no attention to Zack, Special Agent Willow rested his forearms on his thighs and cupped his hands together. "You're sure you never saw the man's face?"

She shook her head. "I'm sorry. It was usually dark when he was there. And he always wore a leather mask, like a hood, tied around the throat. There were wide slits cut out for his eyes, and a hole for his mouth. But everything else was concealed. I couldn't even tell you the color of his hair."

"Leather? That's very specific. You sure about that?"

"The material was dark brown, thick, but soft and pliable. If it wasn't leather, it was something similar."

"Soft. You touched the mask?"

Her cheeks tinged a light pink. "No, Agent Willow. The mask touched me, when *he* touched me." Her words were short, clipped, angry.

Zack winced at the words that she *wasn't* saying. She'd avoided sharing intimate details about her treatment so far. But she was getting closer and closer to telling them *exactly* what the man had done to her. And it was taking every ounce of control that Zack had to keep from putting his arms around her to protect her from having to relive that horror again.

Willow had the grace to look uncomfortable and cleared his throat. "You said he kept you in a box most of the time. What kind of box? Cardboard? Wood?"

"Plexiglas. And before you ask, yes, I'm sure. If it was real glass, I'd have broken it. God knows I tried." She wrung her hands, massaging them, perhaps remembering how they'd hurt as she'd slammed her palms against the top of the box, trying to get out of it.

Zack remembered this part from an earlier interview, and it still made his hands fist at his sides and nausea roll in his stomach. She'd basically been buried alive, kept in a box the size of a coffin, surrounded by dirt walls, able to see the sky above on the rare occasions when the man removed the heavy black cloth that covered the top of the box most of the time. Small holes drilled into the Plexiglas allowed just enough air flow to keep her alive.

The man who'd imprisoned her had sometimes left her in the box for days at a time, without food or water. It was a wonder she hadn't baked to death. There must have been branches overhead, helping to block the heat of the sun. When he did take her out, it was usually at night, or at times when the sun was just beginning to rise or set. She rarely got to see sunlight.

He mainly took her out to give her food and water, just enough to keep her hydrated and fed to the point where she wouldn't die. He forced her to clean the box. And when he wanted to…play…to do whatever sick and twisted things he did to her…he would make her clean herself. While he watched. Anything more than that, including how she'd managed to escape her captor, was anyone's guess. Because every time they got to that part of the interview, she'd shut down.

Willow pulled out the little pocket notebook where he'd made notes earlier when they'd covered this same ground. "You said the box was in the ground, that you could see dirt surrounding you on all sides. But the top was left open?"

Her hands began to shake and she gripped them together in her lap. "Not open. Closed, locked, but covered with a heavy black cloth most of the time. He almost never took the cover off when the sun was up. When he did remove it, his face was concealed behind a mask. That's what gave me hope, that he didn't want me to see his face. I thought… I thought he'd eventually let me go." She swallowed hard and looked down at her lap. "But I found out otherwise, after he brought Mary and shoved her into the box with me. I knew he was going to kill me soon." She shivered. "Mary was my replacement."

"Why did you think she was your replacement?" Willow asked. "Was it because she didn't have her own box?"

She shook her head. "No. I'd tr-tried to escape once before, and he was furious about that. After he…punished me for…defying him, things only got worse. Once M…Mary showed up, he promised he was going to k…kill me."

And this was where the interview had stopped the last time, and the time before that. She started to shake. Her mouth worked but no more words would come. No matter how Willow phrased his questions about Mary, about what happened after that, about how she escaped, she shut down. Her eyes took on a horrified, faraway look as if she were retreating into herself, going somewhere they couldn't reach her.

The therapist motioned to the nurse, who hurried over and checked Kaylee's pulse. Zack knew what was next. They'd call a halt to the questions. And another day would end without them having any more clues that might help them narrow their search, or give them a new lead to follow. He tried not to be aggravated, or let his disappointment show. Because the pale, young woman a few feet away from him was just as much of a victim as Mary.

With one exception.

Kaylee had managed to escape. She'd survived. And Mary deserved that same opportunity. If they could just get Kaylee to answer all of their questions, maybe they could save Mary, too.

Just when it looked as if the nurse was going to wheel Kaylee back to her room, Willow held his hand out to stop her and leaned forward. "You know, Miss Brighton. For the life of me I can't understand why an attractive and intelligent woman such as you would decide to tour the Everglades by herself. Everyone knows the woods are dangerous. Yet you chose to go on that path alone, without a weapon. Why would a pretty girl like you do that?"

His tone was so condescending, so accusatory that Zack's mouth fell open. Everyone stared at the FBI agent in shock, including Kaylee. Willow might be impatient most of the time, but Zack never would have pegged him as one of those people who would blame the victim. As if by virtue of being beautiful, and a woman, she shouldn't have the audacity to walk somewhere by herself without expecting that someone might attack her. Zack was about to tell the agent exactly where he could shove his questions when Kaylee leaned forward with her fists on her knees, glaring at Willow.

"I was in a public area, taking the same path any number of tourists take every single day," Kaylee gritted out. "It's my right as a human being—regardless of how *pretty* I am, Special Agent Willow—to walk anywhere that I want with the expectation of being safe. I shouldn't have to always travel in a group like a pack animal to avoid being attacked."

The nurse leaned down but Kaylee waved her back, never taking her gaze off Willow. "I'm staying right here. I want to hear what Special Agent Willow has to say."

The agent shrugged. "I'm just trying to understand

why you decided to go to that particular part of the Glades. Alone. It's a simple question."

"Then I'll give you a simple answer, and hope you can grasp it." Anger hardened her voice. "I always take a week's vacation from my job at the bank around this time every year. My travel agent suggested some of the recreation areas off Alligator Alley might be a fun diversion before I went to the condo she'd rented for me in Naples."

He poised his pen over a page in his notebook. "What's your travel agent's name?"

She blinked. "I don't see where that matters." Her voice still shook with anger, but she was engaged once again, no longer ready to end the questioning.

Had that been the agent's intent all along when he'd asked that outrageous question? Was it part of his strategy? To make her angry so her fears would fade? Zack glanced at Cole, whose brows were raised as he, too, studied the agent.

"It's just a question," Willow said, his voice neutral, with none of the accusatory tone he'd used before.

Kaylee blew out an impatient breath. "Her name is Sandy Gonzalez. She works for Aventuras Travel Agency based out of Miami. She's handled my family's travel plans for years, decades."

"And the reason you decided to vacation alone?"

"How are these questions going to help you find

those missing women?" She sounded more perplexed than angry this time.

"Could you answer the question, please?"

She jerked her robe tighter over her hospital gown. "No. I can't. I just spent ninety-three days of my life being controlled by a monster. Everything I ate, drank, every move I made, was dictated by him. I've done nothing wrong, Agent Willow. And in spite of what you're implying, I didn't bring any of this on myself." She waved her hand in the air. "Somewhere out there is a monster who's holding Mary Watkins and doing unspeakable things to her. Instead of thinly veiled accusations posed as questions, blaming me for what that man did to me, why aren't you out in the swamp right now searching for her? And that other woman you said was missing?"

He straightened in his chair. "Miss Brighton, my apologies if I sound accusatory. And I know that my questions might seem like a waste of time to you, but this is how we figure things out. We gather as much information as we can about a crime, no matter how trivial, because you never know what the one thing will be that points us in the direction we need to go. As for searching for the missing women, we have teams out in the swamp right now looking for them. They've been out there every day since Chief Scott found you. So I assure you, any time we spend with you isn't taking away from the search. It's my hope that if I ask enough questions, then something you know—that you don't even realize you know—will help us figure out how the man who hurt you targeted you and the others, and where he may be right now. Again, my apologies if I offended you in any way."

Son of a... Zack shook his head. He'd completely misjudged Special Agent Willow. The man's bedside manner might suck, and he was treating Kaylee far more harshly than Zack was comfortable with, but he'd gotten exactly what he wanted. He'd shaken Kaylee out of her stupor and stopped her from retreating into herself and ending the interview like she had always done before. Which must have been his intention all along.

The decision to engage the feds had been Zack's. And he'd been regretting that decision since the minute he'd met Special Agent Willow and took an instant, instinctual dislike to the man. But now, well, he had a renewed respect for him, even if he didn't agree with his methods.

Relaxing his stance, Zack settled in a nearby chair to listen to Willow resume his questioning.

Chapter Six

Three weeks.

It had been three weeks—twenty-one long, tortu-ous days—since Kaylee had fled the never-ending questions of the task force in Naples and had gone home. Or, rather, she'd gone back to her *parents'* home, in Miami Beach. And since she still couldn't deal with the thought of being alone and vulnerable in her apartment in downtown Miami, she was here to stay, for the foreseeable future.

Thinking back to the barrage of questions, day after day, from Special Agent Willow and detectives from both Broward and Collier County, she shivered and rubbed her hands up and down her bare arms. The only one not to pepper her with endless questions was the man who'd become something of a guardian angel the whole time she'd been in the hospital—Police Chief Zack Scott.

He'd made no secret of his disgust over what had amounted to daily interrogations, where she was treated more like a criminal than an innocent victim. Zack had taken up for her, pushing back against all the pressure and siding with the therapist who insisted that Kaylee needed time to heal. The more they questioned her, the more her mind had shut down, muddying her memories.

It wasn't long before the only thing she could remember about her ordeal was being rescued by Zack. The therapist said it was her mind's way of protecting itself from the trauma that she'd suffered, and that if the police didn't stop their questions, they might permanently destroy the very memories they were trying to recover. Which meant that any potential Kaylee might have for helping them find Mary would be lost. That was the only reason she'd agreed to do what her parents, and her doctors, kept begging her to do—go home.

So here she was, starting day twenty-two standing in the kitchen watching her mother put a pork roast and seasonings into a slow cooker for tonight's dinner. Later her mother would combine black beans, onions, garlic and green peppers in a pressure cooker. And once the roast and beans were ready, she would dish them over white rice with plantains and warm, crusty bread on the side. It was a traditional Cuban dish that Kaylee loved.

Her mother had made a point of cooking one of Kaylee's favorite dishes every single night since Kaylee had come home. Which only served to remind her *why* her mother was treating her so extra special these days, and why her father kept his nose buried in his old-fashioned print newspapers in the family room, afraid to say more than a few words to her.

Because of what that monster had done to her in the Everglades.

She shivered in spite of the overheated kitchen. Her decision months ago to call Sandy, her family's long-time travel agent, and book a vacation touring the Glades and Naples had been an ill-fated one. A week off from her job had turned into a nightmare on a path through the marsh when she'd been tackled from behind then gagged, blindfolded and thrown into the trunk of the devil's car.

Her hands clenched into fists on top of the marble countertop. In the family room opposite the kitchen, her father peered at her over this morning's copy of the *Miami Herald*, his gaze dropping to her fists. She forced her hands to relax and faked a smile for his benefit. Relief flickered in his eyes and he lifted the paper again, no doubt feeling that he'd done his duty. He'd checked on her. Never mind that he so easily accepted the front that she put on.

Resentment twisted inside her. This was nothing new—her father avoiding any kind of conflict or show of emotion, her mother busying herself with domestic chores, desperately trying to pretend that everything was okay. Because that was what her parents did, what they had always done. They avoided anything remotely painful, even if that meant pretending their only child had never been abducted and that nothing all that bad had happened to her.

But could Kaylee really blame them? They'd suffered so much loss in their lives, so much heartache in their decades-long attempts to have a child. After four miscarriages they'd finally managed one successful pregnancy. But during the delivery, the cord had wrapped around the baby's throat. The emergency C-section had come too late.

Years passed before they decided to try again for a child, this time through adoption. They'd welcomed Kaylee into their family and loved her as their own, even though she wasn't the infant they'd originally planned on and was instead a troubled girl of five with a habit of throwing tantrums. Under their patient, loving care, she'd blossomed into a confident, happy child, overcoming the abusive past that had landed her in foster care to begin with. And she owed them a tremendous debt for that. So even though her heart ached with the need to talk to them about her ordeal, she held it back, knowing it could very well destroy them.

And also, because they'd never asked.

To an outsider, that might seem cold, callous. But she understood her mom and dad like no one else. They were both old enough to be her grandparents, having decided to pursue adoption when they were well past their prime. Which had only served to make the adoption much more difficult. It had taken many years and expensive lawyers to convince the state to declare them as fit parents in spite of their age and to let an adoption go through.

All the time that had passed, all those terrible losses and struggles, had taken their toll. Neither of them were at the peak of health anymore—Dad with his heart troubles, Mom with her COPD that had her out of breath and on inhalers or oxygen half the time, or laid up sick with bronchitis or pneumonia the rest of the time. Which was why, when her parents had come to her hospital room in Naples, she'd made sure that no one told them the truth about what had happened to her.

It was better to lie, to let them believe a sanitized version of the truth, that she'd been held against her will, yes, but that her captor hadn't really hurt her. Lying to them was her way of protecting the fragile bubble of happiness they'd built around their lives. So she held the truth in.

No matter how much it hurt.

As she watched her mother press the garlic for the black beans, dark, jagged edges of memories battered at her. For several nights in a row, the previously forgotten haunting images of her time in the Glades had been coming back with a vengeance. It was as if a switch had been flipped. Now that her body had recovered, and she wasn't being constantly questioned, her mind was recovering, too. It was re-trieving horrific images that had her waking soaked with sweat, her nails digging so hard into her palms that they drew blood.

The memories were still disjointed, fragments, like looking at a pile of puzzle pieces—each one vivid and clear. But the picture they would form together was still elusive, beyond her grasp. And even though she desperately wanted to forget each of those sharp little pieces of memory, instead she forced herself to think about them and try to put them together into a cohesive whole. Because those memories could be the key to capturing her abductor, the man who'd taken Mary Watkins and very likely the other missing woman, Sue Ellen Fullerton. He could be torturing both of them right now.

Just as he'd tortured *her.*

She drew a ragged breath. Even though she'd vowed not to tell her parents what had really happened, the compulsion this morning, after a particularly rough night, was too strong to ignore. She opened her mouth to spill at least some of the truth. But her mother turned away to get some peppers out of the refrigerator. Seeing her mother's gnarled, arthritic hands shake ever so slightly had Kaylee pressing her lips together. No, she couldn't tell them. So who *could* she confide in?

Certainly not her friends. She couldn't stand the looks of pity that they'd given her upon her return from the hospital, or the shocked whispers when they'd asked about her bruises, her cuts, the ligature marks still visible on her wrists and ankles. They were young, immature, self-centered. Exactly as *she* had naively been before that fateful trip to the Everglades. But where they were still happily going on with their endless parties and frivolous shopping expeditions funded by their parents' money, she no longer shared those interests. And her friends were already drifting away. They didn't stop by anymore, or call. The last text she'd received was at least a week ago, and she was pretty sure she wouldn't get any more.

The only person left with whom she could share her emerging memories was the therapist that her parents had hired here in Miami. And yet, every afternoon when she drove into town to sit in a glass-and-concrete office to meet with her, she couldn't speak, couldn't tell the woman anything about the dark, swirling thoughts that threatened to consume her. Sharing such personal, intimate details with a stranger charging by the hour just didn't feel right.

Kaylee doubted that any amount of therapy could ever "fix" her. Nothing could turn back the clock to the way her life had once been. The ninety-three days she'd spent in the marsh had forever changed her. And she was still struggling to figure out who she was and how to go on. More than anything she wanted to be strong again, to walk down a street without watching over her shoulder or starting at every sound. She wanted to be normal again, to stop being a victim.

But how could she get on with her life when she'd failed to save the other woman being held with her? Here Kaylee was, in the lap of luxury, with the delicious smells of a home-cooked meal filling her nostrils, while Mary was hungry, filthy, suffering hellish torture—if she was even still alive.

Nausea and self-disgust churned in her stomach. She shoved away from the counter.

Her mother's startled glance flicked up from the slow cooker she was stirring. "Kaylee, is something wrong, sweetheart?"

Is something wrong? The question was so absurd that she almost burst into laughter. Instead, she forced another stupid smile.

"Of course not." She sniffed. "Dinner smells great, Mom. Can't wait until tonight." She gave her a gentle hug.

Her mother smiled and patted her shoulder. "You're looking pale, dear. You should sit by the pool today. Relax. Get a tan."

I'm pale because I spent three months in a box, buried alive. Ask me about it, Mama. Ask me what that man did to me.

But her mother didn't ask. She turned to her cooking, to her safe, easy, normal life where bad men didn't slice open daughters, or beat them until they couldn't move or…worse.

"Right. A tan. That's exactly what I need," she muttered, ignoring her mother's questioning look as she headed into the family room. She swiped her phone from the coffee table, ignoring her father peering at her again over his paper, and headed out the sliders at the back of the house.

Plopping down onto one of the lounge chairs by the pool, she held her phone in her hand and started to punch the number for information, to ask them to connect her to the Collier County Sheriff's Office. But then she stopped. Could she do it? Could she really sit in a room full of cops again and relive the horrific images that kept flowing through her mind, share the horrible things that man had done to her? The last time she'd tried, she'd ended up practically comatose, unable to function. And it had taken weeks for her to climb back out of that dark hole. What would happen if she tried again?

What would happen...to Mary...if she didn't?

Her hands started to shake. She set the phone in her lap and wrapped her arms around her middle, rocking back and forth, back and forth, just as she had as a child when the memories of abuse threatened to overwhelm her. Just as she did every time the stress of life got to be too much. And she knew, if she didn't get her fears under control, she'd end up lying on the floor in a fetal position, helpless. Like the victim everyone thought she was.

No. Stop it. You can do this. You have to do this. But how?

One word came to her as clearly as if it had been spoken in a gentle, deep, soothing voice.

Zack.

Just the thought of his kind eyes, his gentle touch, began to calm her, made her hands stop shaking. She knew that she'd fixated on him because he'd saved her from the monster. At least, that was what both the therapist in Naples and the one here in Miami had told her. But even knowing that her placing him on a pedestal like a superhero, as if he were the one man who could defeat the devil, was her mind's way of feeling safe and secure, she couldn't stop thinking about him. And she suddenly realized that the only way she could do what had to be done was if Zack was with her. And if she could talk just to him, one-on-one, without that intimidating FBI agent invading her space, maybe she really could help this time.

An eerie calm settled over her once she'd made her decision. Now, all she had to do was make it happen.

She picked up her phone again then glanced over her shoulder to make sure that the sliding glass doors were still closed, that her mother hadn't silently drifted out onto the pool deck to check on her. Her mom might not want to confront Kaylee's recent, traumatic past head-on. But she showed her concern in other ways, by hovering, watching, as if she could keep her only daughter safe by tracking her movements from room to room. The attention was given with love, but it could also be stifling, which made

Kaylee's decision even easier. However, before calling Zack, she called another number that was programmed into her phone.

"Aventuras Travel Agency, Sandy Gonzalez speaking." The cheery voice came on the line.

"Sandy, this is Kaylee Brighton."

"Kaylee. My God. I… I've wanted to call you, ever since I saw the story in the news. But I wasn't sure… that is, I don't… I just wanted to say that I'm sorry. I never meant for any of this to—"

"Stop, stop, please." Kaylee let out a shaky breath. "What happened to me is in no way your fault. You couldn't have known what would happen when you scheduled that trip for me. And I feel terrible if your business has suffered because of all of the publicity. Honestly, I don't know how the local papers got a hold of the fact that I'd even booked my trip through you. I couldn't believe it when I saw them talking about it on the front page, as if no one should use your agency. I swear I never told them anything. I've never even spoken to the media. And I—"

"Kaylee, hold it. Do *not* apologize to me for anything. Goodness, I would never blame you or think you were behind the bad press. Put that thought right out of your mind. No worries, all right? Is that why you called? You were worried about my company? Because, trust me, that's the last thing that I want you concerned about."

"No, that's not why I called. Although I really *should* have called, as soon as I saw that story."

"Honey," Sandy said, "I'm the one who should have called. I wanted to. But I didn't want to bring up any bad memories. Are you…are you okay…now?"

Okay. Again she felt like laughing in a rather hysterical kind of way. But Sandy wouldn't understand. Kaylee wasn't even sure that *she* understood.

"I'm…fine." There. That sounded convincing and normal, didn't it?

"Good, I'm so glad. Is there…is there something that I can do for you?"

"Yes, actually. There is." She told the agent what she wanted. Sandy's startled exclamation had Kaylee wincing and pulling the phone away from her ear. "Yes, yes, I'm sure. And this needs to be between you and me. My parents can't hear about this. I'm… going to tell them I'm staying with a friend. That I need some space. They won't worry about me if they think I'm with someone."

"I don't like it," Sandy said. "But if you're going to do this, then there's something I absolutely insist on."

After several minutes of arguing and negotiating, Kaylee gave up the fight and agreed to Sandy's stipulations. Once the arrangements were made, she hung up and called a number she didn't have to dial information to request. She'd memorized it, a cell phone number given to her in the hospital.

By Zack.

Her pulse sped up at the thought of hearing his voice again, but not because he was handsome or was exactly the type of man she would have been attracted to in her former life. She didn't care about handsome anymore, not after…not after what she'd been through. She doubted she'd ever care again about things like that. No, her pulse thrummed because of how he made her feel—safe, secure and as if she could do anything, like fight the devil and win.

The line clicked. "Detective Larson, may I help you?"

Not the voice she'd been hoping to hear.

"I'm sorry." She tried to hide her disappointment. "I must have called the wrong number. I'm trying to reach Chief Scott."

A pause, then "Miss Brighton? Is that you?"

Caught. "Yes. Could you please give me Chief Scott's number? I thought I was calling his cell but obviously I've called yours instead. I need to talk to him."

"You called the right number. He left me his phone in case someone needed to get in touch with him in an emergency. There is no cell service where he is right now. His phone was sitting on my desk and rang, so I picked it up."

"Oh. Well, I don't know that I'd call this an emergency, but it's very important. I'd appreciate it if you would tell him that I need to talk to him and—"

"Miss Brighton, I'm sorry, but unless it's urgent I

really can't justify interrupting the work that Zack's doing on the Ghost of Mystic Glades case just to tell him to—"

"You're calling the man who abducted me a ghost? Why? He's the devil, not a ghost. I didn't *imagine* what he did to me. He—"

"Miss Brighton, hold on. I'm really, really sorry. I shouldn't have said that. It came out before I could stop it." He let out a deep sigh. "Believe me, no one is trying to belittle your experience by assigning a cutesy name to the killer. It's just that there's a legend in the Glades…well, it doesn't matter. What I was trying to say is that I'd prefer to take care of whatever you're calling about rather than drive out to find Chief Scott. I'm part of the same task force that he's on trying to bring the man to justice who hurt you. That *is* why you called, right? To tell me something about the case?"

She pressed her hand against her chest, embarrassed at her outburst. "Detective, forgive me. I shouldn't have jumped all over you like that. I get… flustered, and emotional these days."

"You absolutely don't owe me an apology. Now, how can I help you?"

She curled her hand around the phone. "I appreciate your offer, but it's Zack that I need to speak to."

Silence met her request, and she realized her blunder—calling Chief Scott by his first name. Her face grew heated, but there was no backpedaling now. She had no control over what crazy thoughts might be running through the detective's head. And she didn't care about all the reasons her therapist gave her for what she called her *fixation* on the man who'd saved her. To her, Chief Scott would always be Zack. And Zack was the only person she felt comfortable enough to talk to about what had happened.

"If you'll leave your message with me, I promise that I'll give it to him the minute I go home to Mystic Glades this evening. He'll have to stop the search at nightfall."

There was a slight intake of breath on the line, and she realized he'd said more than he'd intended. Her pulse hammered in her veins as dreaded images pounded through her mind like a battering ram, making her temples throb.

"He's...he's out *there*? In the swamp? Looking for her?"

A deep sigh sounded. "Yes. Zack is searching for both of them, Mary Watkins and Sue Ellen Fullerton. Like I said, if you'll just give me the message, I promise I'll tell him tonight—"

"No. That will be too late. You need to tell him now."

Another sigh, this one of resignation. "All right. Give me your message."

"You'll take it to him right now? You won't wait until later? Promise?"

"I promise." His voice sounded weary, but it also sounded honest. She believed him.

"Okay. Please tell him that I remember… I remember… Things are coming back. I need to talk to him. I…" She drew a shaky breath. "I think I can help him find Mary now."

"Miss Brighton…" His voice took on an edge of excitement and impatience. "Are you saying that you can tell us the location where you were held?"

"Not exactly. But I feel… I *know*…that if I go out there, where Zack found me, the rest will follow. The details will come. I want to help find Mary. And the only way that I can do that is to go to the swamp and see if being there will make the pieces of my memory come together and make sense."

Disappointment was heavy in his sigh and the long moment of silence that followed. Maybe she should have said she definitely knew where to find Mary instead of being honest. But she really did believe the fragments of memories that were barraging her would form a complete picture if she could just get back to the swamp. But she couldn't do it alone. She needed someone with her, someone she could trust to keep her safe, and grounded. She needed Zack.

"Detective—"

"I appreciate that you want to help. I really do. But unless you know the exact location, unless you're positive of where Mary is, I think that going against your therapist's advice is too risky. I remember she was adamant that the only safe way for you to recover the chunks of your missing memories is in a safe, controlled environment—specifically, your therapist's office. Coming here isn't recommended and is why you left in the first place. I couldn't live with myself if something…bad…happened to you because we went against your doctor's orders. Especially if we have a real chance of you remembering everything, but by coming here too soon, you go backward and forget it all. Can you understand my hesitancy?"

She curled her hands around the phone in frustration. She was so tired of other people telling her what to do, of thinking they knew what was best for her.

"Let's cut to the chase, Detective." Frustration made her voice harsher than she'd intended. She cleared her throat and tried to keep her voice even. "I've been keeping up with the investigation through the news channels, and it's clear that you have no leads. Isn't that right?"

"I wouldn't say we have *no* leads," he hedged.

"I think I deserve the truth. Do you have any leads or not?"

Another long silence, then "No. We don't."

"Then I suggest that you get in touch with Zack right away. Tell him that I'm ready to face the devil. I'm flying to Naples Municipal Airport this morning. And I want Zack to pick me up, so he can take me to the Everglades to the exact spot where he… where he found me."

"You're flying in from Miami? I didn't think they even had flights from there to here. It's only a few hours' drive."

"A friend hired a private plane for me."

What she didn't tell him was that Sandy had insisted on the rather extravagant gesture. The travel agent had astutely realized that Kaylee dreaded driving the same trek she'd driven the last time she'd gone to Naples, a trip that had ended with her in a box in the ground. Just getting on the plane was going to be difficult. The only way she felt she could face it was knowing that Zack would be there on the other side. Zack would keep her safe.

"Your mind's already made up. You're coming out here no matter what, aren't you?"

"Yes."

When he didn't immediately agree to her request, she played the card she'd held back just in case. She already hated herself for what she was about to say, but she really was desperate.

"Detective, if you won't help me, if you won't get Zack to pick me up at the airport and then take me out to the swamp to look for Mary, I'm afraid I'll have to take my plight to the press. And I'm pretty sure they won't report favorably about the Collier County Sheriff's Office once they hear that you refused to let the only witness help you find Mary, before it's too late."

His voice was clipped and angry when he replied. "What time should I tell Zack to pick you up?"

Chapter Seven

Zack cursed beneath his breath as he strode through the large glass doors into Naples Municipal Airport. People gave him curious looks as he passed them, no doubt because of his muddy shoes and dirt-smeared clothes. The filthy hair probably didn't help either. He'd fallen more than a few times in the marsh today, and it seemed like half the swamp had ended up in his hair or his mouth at one point or another. If he didn't catch some kind of disease by the time this was over it would be a miracle. But it wasn't the fear of catching a disease that had him so aggravated. It was the fact that he'd had to stop searching for the missing women and waste precious daylight to pick up Kaylee Brighton at the airport.

A pang of guilt knocked the edge off his temper. She was, after all, a victim. She'd gone through unbelievable horrors at the hands of the same man that he was trying to catch. And if it wasn't for her bravery in risking everything to get away from her captor, Zack and the others wouldn't even know to look for

Mary or Sue Ellen. But still, she was safe and sound with her wealthy parents in Miami. Or should have been. She had no business coming back, not this soon.

He remembered the therapist that the victims' advocate group had brought in, telling them all how fragile she was. Pushing Kaylee too fast, too soon, could destroy not only the memories they hoped to use to help them in the case, but her, as well. He hadn't expected her to contact them for at least a few more months. And he'd desperately hoped he'd have already found Mary and Sue Ellen alive and well long before then, and she wouldn't need to come back.

He didn't see how anything good could come from taking him away from the search, or involving Kaylee. Which was why he was going to stop her, turn her around and tell her to get back on that private jet of hers and return to Miami.

Private jet. He shook his head. Kaylee Brighton had all the advantages in life—or at least, she had, before her harrowing experience. She had access to the best doctors that money could buy. Her responsibility right now was to use those advantages to help her heal. She shouldn't be flying out here on a whim and interfering with his efforts to find those missing women. And he was going to tell her exactly that when he saw her.

But then he saw her.

Fifty feet away, looking lost, frightened, her face incredibly pale in contrast to her shoulder-length dark hair as she headed toward him, pulling a rolling suit-case. Her purse was clutched against her flat belly, her wide eyes darting all around as if she was afraid one of the people in the crowd might grab her and drag her off somewhere to torture her.

Zack's shoulders slumped. He stopped where he was, berating himself for his earlier unkind thoughts. This wasn't some spoiled little rich girl wanting to be the center of attention. And she wasn't here to pur-posely interfere with his search. No one who looked that scared, that…bleak, would come here except for one reason—to help them with the investigation, just as Cole had told Zack when Cole had driven out to the search site an hour earlier.

Now he wished he'd taken a few minutes to change his clothes and wash the filth of the marsh off his body before driving to the airport. He didn't want to frighten her even more, or bring back horrific memo-ries of what had happened to her because of his knee-jerk reaction to her demanding that he pick her up.

He eyed the door to the men's room not too far away, wondering if he could quickly clean himself up enough to make a difference. But it was too late. She'd already spotted him. And the look of intense relief that washed over her delicate features had him feel-ing guilty all over again for even considering making her wait while he washed.

Hurrying forward, he schooled his expression into one of patience instead of the impatient, angry expression he knew he must have worn before. They stopped a few feet from each other, the crowd parting like rapids around a boulder as he debated whether or not to shake her hand. He didn't want to frighten her. The decision was taken from him when she reached out, not with one hand, but both hands, and wrapped them around his waist.

"Thank God you came." Her voice sounded ragged. "Thank you."

His shock turned to guilt again as he gently put his arms around her, holding her against his chest. Her whole body was shaking. And it was only then that he realized how traumatic it must have been for her to take the flight out here and brave the crowds of strangers in the airport.

"Come on." He urged her toward the wall and away from the steady stream of people. "Do you have more luggage we need to pick up?"

"N…no. Just this." She pulled away from him, gave him a watery smile and motioned toward her carry-on. "I'm not even sure what I brought. I just tossed things in until it was full and left."

"May I?" He moved his hand toward the suitcase handle but waited for her permission. She seemed so fragile, like a doe that might bolt if he made any sudden moves.

"Um, sure. Okay. Thank you." Her eyes flitted past him, taking in their surroundings.

"Kaylee?"

"Yes?" She sounded distracted as she watched the people walk past.

"You can let go of the handle now."

She looked down at her hand on her suitcase then let go. "I'm...I'm sorry." She squared her shoulders before looking up at him again. Some of the fear had left her eyes, and in its place was a look he hadn't seen in her before...determination. "I really am sorry. About interfering with your search. I promise I wouldn't have done so if I could have...if I could... do this by myself." She motioned to the crowd moving past them. "I'm still...uneasy...around strangers." She fisted her hands at her sides. "I just... I want to help. I know I can help. But I'm not strong enough yet to do it on my own. If you're with me, I know I can do this, help you find Mary."

As she stared up at him with such complete trust and faith, he felt something crack open inside, letting her in where he'd never let anyone else in since losing Jo Lynne all those years ago.

And that scared the hell out of him.

He had a job to do, an incredibly important one. There were lives at stake. He couldn't let this beautiful, fragile woman distract him from what needed to be done. And somehow he had to break this...bond... or whatever it was, that had struck up between them since the moment he'd held her broken body on that road and felt her hand clutch his.

"We need to go." Steeling himself against the hurt

look that flickered across her face, he turned toward the exit, pulling her suitcase behind him. "It's going to rain again soon. We need to hurry or we'll get soaked."

"There's been a lot of rain around here from what I've seen on the news." She was slightly out of breath, probably from keeping pace with his much longer legs.

He slowed down to match her shorter stride. "It's wreaked havoc on our search, I can tell you that."

They exited through automatic sliding glass doors and he gestured toward his dark blue four-by-four pickup truck parked at the curb about thirty feet to the right with Collier County Deputy Holder standing outside it, arguing with a TSA agent. From the relieved look on Holder's face when he saw Zack, he was obviously losing the argument.

"Here he is right now," Holder told the TSA guard. "This is Chief Zack Scott."

Zack smiled at the agent and shook his hand, acutely aware that Kaylee had sucked in a breath and stopped slightly behind him. She probably hadn't expected him to bring another cop with him. But there was nothing he could do about that now. He'd fully expected it would only take a few minutes to convince her to hop back on her plane and go home. And since Deputy Holder had been paired up with him today to conduct the search of the grid that they'd been assigned, they'd driven to the airport together, rather than leave Holder by himself. They were using the buddy system while searching, acutely aware that they were looking for an extremely dangerous killer, and not wanting any officers isolated and alone, vulnerable to an ambush.

After soothing the ruffled feathers of the TSA agent and promising not to park in front of the airport like that again, even with a deputy in the car, Zack gestured toward the rear door of the king cab. "Mind sitting back there, Holder? Miss Brighton will sit up front with me."

"No problem."

Holder nodded at Kaylee when Zack introduced them. As the deputy got into the backseat and took the suitcase, he gave Zack a questioning look. All Zack could do was shrug. How could he explain to the other man *why* he'd given in and let Kaylee come along with them when he didn't understand it himself?

He held open the front passenger door, expecting Kaylee to step up inside. But instead, she stood frozen on the sidewalk, her face as pale as ever. Immediately on alert, Zack turned around, scanning the people and vehicles near them. But he didn't see anything alarming—except for the TSA agent staring at them, crossing his arms and waiting for the truck to get moving.

"Miss Brighton… Kaylee, we need to go."

A shiver went through her body as she stared at the truck's front bumper. And that was when Zack realized his blunder. In his rush to get to the airport and convince Kaylee to hop on the next plane to Miami, he hadn't even considered the possibility that he'd be taking her back with him.

In the same truck that he'd hit her with when she'd run from her abductor.

He silently cursed himself for being such an idiot. He could practically see her thoughts flashing across her expressive face. She was valiantly trying to gather her courage, stiffening her spine.

"Kaylee." He kept his voice low, gentle. "It's just a truck, okay? I promise it's safe. And I'm so, so sorry that I didn't think to bring a different vehicle. If you want, I can have Deputy Holder drive it back and we can take a cab." He turned to do just that, wave down a cab, but her soft, warm fingers curled around his forearm.

"No, wait." Her hand tightened on his arm. "I'm sorry. You're right. It's just a truck." She gave him a brave smile that was barely above a grimace. "I'll be okay. Let's go."

He was determined to get a cab but she moved past him and hopped up into the passenger seat. Since the TSA agent was striding toward them again and Zack knew he wouldn't get off easy this time, he closed the door then hurriedly got into the driver's side. He squealed the tires pulling away from the curb, leaving a very angry agent behind on the sidewalk, with his hands on his hips.

Beside him, Kaylee sat stiff and silent. He wished he could think of something to make her feel better, but they weren't that far from their destination. So he figured the best thing to do now was just bite the bullet and get there as quickly as he could.

A few minutes later he was heading north on Airport Pulling Road. And a few minutes after that he slowed and put his blinker on to signal his turn onto Mercantile Avenue.

Kaylee sat up straighter in her seat, her brows crinkling. "Wait, why are you turning? The sign to I-75 says to continue north on this road."

"We're not going to the interstate." He made the turn.

She jerked her head toward him. "Isn't that where you're searching for Mary? Off Alligator Alley?"

"Yes."

"I don't understand. Where are we going?"

"Here." He turned into the parking lot in front of the Collier County Sheriff's Office.

THERE WERE 2,304 little one-inch squares in the grid pattern in the safety glass on the conference room wall opposite from where Kaylee was sitting. At least, if her math skills were right, and 48 squares up times 48 squares across equaled what she thought it did. In the middle of all that glass was the round seal of the Collier County Sheriff's Office, with red, blue and green arrows displaying the words "Community, Safety, Service."

Looking away from the glass, she leaned back in her chair and studied the yellowing ceiling above her. Counting the acoustic tiles had been a little more difficult than counting the grid pattern in the glass window because the room was L-shaped. The short leg of the L was at the far end. It boasted a vending machine with all kinds of chips and candy, and two rows of expired "healthy" energy bars. Apparently, the cops preferred the chips, because they hadn't been allowed to expire.

There was also a narrow cabinet and countertop beside the machine, with a coffeemaker and microwave. If her assumption was correct that the ceiling tiles in the little L each constituted one-third of a full tile, then overall there were 105 tiles.

She shoved back from the table and contemplated the swirls in the carpet. There was probably a pattern there, too, hidden amongst the coffee stains and dark impressions where many a booted foot had probably shuffled restlessly under the table, waiting for another boring meeting to end. Of course, none of their meetings could be as boring as hers—a meeting for one—while she waited for Zack to return from wherever he'd gone.

In spite of her protests, he'd escorted her through the lobby of the sheriff's office, down a long tan hallway filled with crayon drawings on the wall, probably from one of the neighborhood elementary schools, and into the conference room.

And then he'd left.

That was—she looked at her watch—forty-five minutes ago. She ran a finger over the tiny diamonds that marched around the delicate gold face. This watch was a replacement for the original one that her parents had gifted her on her sixteenth birthday: the watch the devil had taken from her the day he'd abducted her.

She shivered and ran her hands up and down her arms. Was Zack punishing her for pulling him off the search? He hadn't seemed the type to be so petty, especially when a woman's life hung in the balance.

The sound of footsteps coming down the long hallway outside the conference room had her focusing on the large glass opening in the opposite wall. A moment later Zack walked past it and opened the door.

"You tricked me," she immediately accused, even as she noticed that his hair was wet and that he'd undergone an amazing transformation since picking her up at the airport. He was clean, wearing clean clothes. Even in her current state of mind, she could appreciate how handsome he was, and how wonderful he smelled. But that didn't make her any less annoyed at him. "You were supposed to take me to the search site."

He rounded the table and stopped beside her, his hand on the back of her chair.

"I never said I'd take you there." His voice was tight, his expression grim.

Something was definitely wrong.

"What happened?" she asked, her earlier annoyance gone. "Zack? Tell me."

He pulled out the chair beside her as more footsteps sounded out in the hallway. The door opened and two men in suits stepped into the room, men she recognized as Lieutenant Shlafer and Detective Larson. A third man came in behind them, but instead of a suit, he wore dark blue pants and a white lab coat.

Zack sat beside her and gave her a sympathetic look.

The suits moved out of the way, letting the man in the lab coat stand front and center. He was holding a clipboard with a sheaf of papers on it. But it was the embroidered words above the right breast pocket on his lab coat that had Kaylee's stomach twisting into a cold, hard knot.

Medical Examiner.

Her gaze flew to Zack. "No. Please. Tell me she's not…" She choked on the words, unable to finish her sentence.

He took her hands in his. "I'm so sorry, Kaylee. They found her while we were at the airport. The ME just finished the confirmation. Mary Watkins is dead."

Chapter Eight

Kaylee collapsed against Zack, her hands fisting in his shirt as she sobbed out her sorrow. He wished he could have softened the blow, eased into telling her about Mary. He hadn't expected Lieutenant Drew Shlafer to bring the ME with him into the conference room. He frowned his displeasure at Drew over the top of Kaylee's head.

"Sorry," Drew mouthed silently, looking embarrassed. Zack's anger drained out of him. He knew that Drew was a good man, and a good boss, at least according to Cole, who actually worked for him. Drew hadn't meant any harm. None of them had. And Zack really couldn't fault them. They were all doing their jobs.

With an investigation that had stalled, they were excited to have Kaylee back, anxious to finally get answers to the questions they'd never been able to ask when she'd been recovering at the hospital. Plus, with at least one more woman's life possibly on the line—assuming that Sue Ellen Fullerton's disappearance was linked to Mary's and Kaylee's—it was understandable that everyone was moving forward at warp speed and not taking the time they might otherwise have taken.

"It's all my fault," Kaylee whispered brokenly against his chest. "It's all my fault."

"Shhh, it's okay. And it's *not* your fault." Running one hand over her dark, silky hair while he lightly stroked her back, he motioned with his chin toward the door. "Guys, give us a few minutes."

Drew ushered the others out. But he paused in the doorway, a worried frown creasing his brow. "We should have handled that better." He hesitated, as if he wanted to say something else.

Zack let out an aggravated breath. He knew what the other man was waiting for. "I'll call you when she's ready to talk."

Relief flashed in the lieutenant's eyes. He closed the door, his dress shoes echoing in the hallway as he headed back to the squad room and his office beyond that.

When Kaylee quit shaking and quieted against him, Zack gently pulled her back, his hands on her shoulders. He looked down into her dark, red-rimmed eyes.

"Can I get you something? Water? A soda?"

She shook her head. "No." She cleared her throat and straightened in her chair. The devastated look on her face gave way to the same grim determination that he'd seen in the airport.

"I'm sorry I soaked your shirt. I'm not usually like this." She laughed bitterly. "Until the past few months, I couldn't have told you the last time that I'd cried. And now I seem to cry all the time. It's ridiculous."

He held out his right hand, palm up, and waited.

She blinked in surprise then put her hand in his.

He linked their fingers together and rested their joined hands on the top of his thigh. "You've been through hell. And still you came back to help with the investigation. That's more than most people would have done. So don't be so hard on yourself. You can cry on me anytime you want." He smiled and was rewarded with her hesitant smile in return, her fingers tightening on his in a soft squeeze before she pulled her hand back.

"Thank you. Again," she said. "You've been so nice to me this whole time. I… I know I've clung to you, literally and figuratively. I don't mean to be such a pain. It's just that… I trust you. Being around you makes me, well, it makes me feel safe, calms me down." She grimaced. "Usually." She ran a shaky hand through her shoulder-length hair, pushing it out of her face and behind her ears. "I should have come back earlier, to help find Mary in time."

"Nothing you could have done would have saved her."

Her eyes flashed with a hint of anger, but it seemed self-directed. "You don't know that."

"Yes. I do. I didn't expect the lieutenant to bring

the medical examiner in here with him. I apologize for that. But everyone was in a hurry to talk to you. And the ME was probably just as anxious as the others to reassure you that you couldn't have saved Mary. Although he's not finished with the autopsy, he did determine time of death. She was killed right around the time that I hit you with my truck, give or take a few hours either way. So you see, there was nothing you could have done. Waiting a few weeks to come back here didn't make a difference."

He expected to see relief in her eyes. Instead, she looked horrified.

"Then I killed her by running away. As soon as he saw you on the road, he must have gone back and—"

"Wait. Hold it." He leaned forward. "Are you saying he was there, by the road, when Cole and I were there with you?"

Her eyes squeezed shut and she nodded, her face a mask of pain. "Yes. That's one of the things that I saw in one of my nightmares. I remember his eyes, staring at me with such hate, such evil, through the holes in the mask as he stood in the bushes at the edge of the road, watching us. He…he took a step toward you. I tried to warn you. And then the other policeman, Cole, drove up. The devil stepped back into the trees. You saved me. But Cole saved you, by arriving at that specific moment."

Zack rather doubted that Cole's arrival had saved him, though he supposed it was possible. He preferred to think that his own instincts and reflexes, his training, were better than that. He would have sensed the man behind him, or heard him approaching, long before the stranger could have hurt him. He just wished he'd known that Kaylee was running from a captor, and that Cole *hadn't* arrived when he did, so Zack would have had a chance to confront and stop the man that Kaylee called the devil.

He *did* remember Kaylee trying to tell him something as she lay in the road, broken and bleeding. But he was so upset over hitting her that he didn't try to get her to repeat anything. He'd just wanted her to be still so she wouldn't make any of her injuries worse before he could get her to a hospital.

If he'd known the circumstances, that she'd been running from a captor, maybe Mary *could* have been saved. But he wasn't going to lay something like that out for Kaylee to think about. She'd only blame herself even more. And the one thing Zack knew beyond a doubt was that the only person to blame for Mary's death was the *animal* who'd killed her.

"How…how did she die?" Kaylee asked, her voice a quiet whisper.

She was beaten, savagely, then strangled. But he wasn't about to dish that out on top of everything she was going through.

"It was quick," he lied. "She didn't suffer."

He stared into her eyes, hoping to convince her that he was telling the truth, hoping he could at least take that one burden away from her. But her sad smile told him that he hadn't fooled her. She gave him a slight nod, letting him know without words that she understood what he was trying to do and that she wouldn't press for details.

"I wish we could have found her in time," she said.

"Sue Ellen is still out there. We still have a chance to save her. And, equally important, we have a chance to stop this man before he abducts anyone else."

She wrapped her hands around her waist. "You're right."

"What else do you remember?" he asked.

"Bits and pieces. I mean, a lot, I remember a lot. Just not necessarily in the right order. I thought that if I came back, if you took me to where you found me, that would help me put everything together to form a timeline that makes sense, to help me backtrack to the last camp where he held us."

"The *last* camp? That implies there have been *other* camps, that he moved around with you. Is that right?"

Her eyes widened in surprise, as if the pieces of her memories were forming that larger whole she'd been hoping for. "Yes. Yes, we did. You're right. You think maybe Sue Ellen is at one of his other camps? That she could still be alive?"

"It's possible."

He studied her profile. It was time to bring the others in, let them question her, see what else she could remember. They had years of training as detectives, whereas his experience was largely in patrol and later as the head of a small squad before becoming "chief of no one" in his fledgling Mystic Glades Police Department. Leaving the detecting to Drew and his team was the smart thing to do. But he had a few more questions of his own to ask before he turned his focus back to the search for the missing woman.

"Kaylee."

She arched a brow in question.

"If the man who held you captive also abducted Mary Watkins, then he must have left you alone while he did that. He must have, what, taken you out of the box and chained you somewhere when he went after his next victim?"

The fingers of her right hand lightly traced the angry, still-healing red scars on her left wrists. "No. Whenever he left me, I was always in the box. Unchained." As if just realizing what she was doing, she stopped rubbing her wrist and rested her hand on top of the table. "The chains were for when he was there, when he took me out of the box. He blindfolded me, tied me up and…"

He got up and headed to the kitchenette at the far end of the room. He returned with a cold bottle of water and a Coke from the mini-fridge and set them in front of her.

"Thank you," she murmured, and took a long pull from the water bottle before setting it down. She pushed her hair behind her ears again and gave him a grim smile. "You don't have to keep treating me like a fragile doll. I'm not going to fall apart like I did right after you rescued me. I may cry a little, or even get angry. But I'm not going back home until I've done everything that I can to find Sue Ellen, and the man who hurt me, who hurt Mary and any other women he may have done this to. So go ahead, ask me whatever questions you're burning to ask. Because it's obvious that there's something else you want to know."

"You're a courageous woman, Kaylee. A lot tougher than I realized when we first met."

"No." She shook her head. "If I were tough, if I were courageous, I wouldn't have run. I'd have figured out another way to defeat him. I wouldn't have left anyone behind."

That, of course, was completely wrong. He knew it, and he imagined she probably did, too, somewhere in the back of her mind beneath all of the guilt that she was piling on herself. But he also knew that she wasn't ready to let go of that guilt, and nothing he said was going to change her mind right now. So instead, he asked the questions that were indeed burning to be asked.

"Can you tell me how often he left you there, alone? How many days passed before you'd see him again?"

"Didn't I answer these questions at the hospital, when Special Agent Willow interviewed me?"

"Some, yes. But I'd like to take you through it again, see if you remember anything new before we get to the really hard part."

She nodded, her hair sliding out from behind her ears. She impatiently pushed it back. "It was difficult to judge the passage of time. But I'm certain he left me alone for two or three days sometimes. It couldn't have been much longer or I'd have died from dehydration. He never left any water or food with me. When he was there, it was usually early in the mornings, when the sun wasn't quite up yet. Or late, when the sun was setting. Sort of like you'd do with a dog, he took me out twice a day so I could relieve myself."

Her face flamed red but she continued the story. "But those were very short bouts of freedom. It was rare that I ever really saw sunlight. Mostly, he took me out late at night. Sometimes I'd be out for hours, with my wrists and legs shackled. My daily chore was to wipe down the box with wet cloths. He always seemed to have whatever supplies he needed—soap, shampoo, water, even freshly washed clothes every few days. He preferred me…clean. Said he wanted me…presentable, pretty."

She swallowed hard and looked away. But the memories haunting her were revealed in the flicker of emotions that flashed across her face—disgust, fear, embarrassment.

"Except for those times, I was always in the box. Well, except for when we moved to another camp.

That was always during the day. He'd grab me up, blindfold and gag me then chain me and throw me in the back of a truck or car. A few hours later the vehicle would stop, he'd untie me and shove me into another box."

Zack stared at her. "Another box? He didn't take the box with him when he moved you?"

Her brows crinkled. "No. Is that significant?"

"Maybe. Did you ever move to the same camps? Or were they always new camps?"

She thought about it a moment then shrugged. "I suppose they could have been the same ones. We moved about once a week. The terrain was always the same—swamps, mud, dirt, cypress and oak trees. Like I said, it was usually dark. The things I saw were by moonlight or firelight."

"Fire? He had a campfire at night?"

She nodded. "Sometimes. That and the occasional flashlight. The trees were always thick—lots of canopy cover overhead."

"You've said he either kept you locked in the box, or chained, right?"

"Yes."

"But you escaped. How?" He held his breath, worried that he might have pushed too far. She'd never told anyone this part in the other interviews.

"The first time…it was stupid, desperation, I guess," she began haltingly. "He took me into the woods to chain me. I think he must have forgotten something, so he went back toward the camp. He must have assumed that I wouldn't move, that I'd wait for him. But I didn't. I ran. Just…ran." She shivered. "He caught me, of course. I was only free for a few minutes. And I paid dearly for my defiance."

The tortured look in her eyes made him want to pull her into his arms. But he needed this information. And he couldn't afford to do anything that might make her stop. Not yet.

"But you tried again. And that time you got away."

She slowly nodded. "It was after he brought Mary to the camp. He opened the box and pulled her out. He was so…consumed with her, that he didn't look at me as he closed the lid. I pressed my hands against the Plexiglas and tapped my nails, once, trying to make him think the clicking noise was the latch, locking it in place." A look of wonder crossed her face. "It worked. I couldn't believe it. He pulled Mary into the trees and I pushed the lid up and crawled out. I closed it behind me, and took off. And left her."

A sob bubbled up in her throat but she waved him away when he would have tried to comfort her. "No. I have to be strong. If I start crying again, I'll be no good to you or the others. Is any of this helping?"

It was helping far more than she realized. But she'd just reminded him of his promise to let Drew know when she was ready to talk. He'd already kept her too long, and he needed to turn her over to the detectives. He rose, but motioned for her to stay seated.

"If you're up for it, I'm going to have Drew and the others return. They want to interview you."

"But I want to help you find Sue Ellen. Aren't you going to take me to the swamp?"

Not a chance. He wasn't going to victimize her by taking her to the scene of the crime. But he could avoid that conversation by telling her a different truth.

"The best way that you can help right now is to answer the detectives' questions. Besides, by the time I could get a new search team organized to take you out there, it'd be getting dark. And it's far too dangerous to be out there at night. None of our searchers stay out past nightfall."

She slumped in her chair, looking dejected. "All right. I'll answer their questions."

"Thanks. I'll let them know."

"Zack?"

He turned at the door.

"Are you being honest when you say the searchers don't stay out after dark?"

"Yes, absolutely."

She studied him, as if weighing his words for truthfulness. "Okay. Then I won't badger you to take me out there today. But I promise you. Nothing's going to stop me from going out there tomorrow. I'd like you to go with me. I'll feel safer that way. But if you refuse, then I'll go with someone else. I'm not bluffing."

Unfortunately, he could tell that she wasn't. He didn't doubt for a second that she'd do exactly what she'd said, head out there by herself if she had to. At first blush, that sounded crazy, reckless. But he understood exactly why she was being so stubborn—survivor's guilt. And he couldn't help but admire and respect that she was willing to risk everything to save a woman she'd never even met. That kind of selflessness and courage were rare in this world. And he had a feeling that was only the tip of the iceberg with Kaylee Brighton.

She was an intriguing woman, full of surprises. He certainly never would have suspected the backbone she had when he'd seen her fragile and scared in the hospital. But just because he respected her reasons for wanting to go out to the swamp and help with the search didn't mean that he'd actually let her go. If he had to, he'd put her in protective custody. No way was she going out there.

He gave her a curt nod. She probably thought he was agreeing to take her searching tomorrow. And he felt a twinge of guilt for allowing her to think that. But it still didn't change his mind.

After closing the door behind him, he hurried past the glass window down the hall to the squad room. He'd let the investigators know that they could interview Kaylee now. But Cole's boss, Drew, would have to wait until Zack had a chance to talk to him before he could join them. Because everything that Kaylee had told him had just clicked together in his mind. And the picture that formed was about to send the investigation in a new direction.

He just hoped that Drew saw the picture the way he did, and agreed with the decision he'd made.

ZACK STOOD IN front of Drew's desk, waiting for his reaction. He didn't have to wait long.

"What do you mean, we're searching in the wrong place?" Drew motioned to the group of detectives in the squad room through the glass door of his office, letting them know to go ahead to the conference room to interview Kaylee without him.

Zack brought Drew up to speed on everything that Kaylee had just told him. Then he hooked his foot on the leg of one of the guest chairs and scooted it over to the front of the desk before plopping down on it.

"We searched the area where we found Kaylee," Zack said. "And came up empty. The rains destroyed any footprints or trail, and there wasn't much to go on. But we did the best we could. We went back for several hours in every direction, going much farther than we thought she could have possibly run with her captor chasing her and still, nothing. We also assumed that the killer wouldn't return to that area since Kaylee had escaped. He'd be a fool to do so, right? So when we didn't find anything, we turned our focus on other areas, close to where the other women were abducted."

"Which yielded Mary Watkins's body, a mile from where she'd last been seen. So what's your point about searching in the wrong spot?"

"My point is that Mary was killed close to the time that I found Kaylee. Which means she had to have been killed in the same area where Kaylee had last been held—not where we found Mary's body. The killer—"

"Moved the body to throw us off."

"Right. He didn't want her found anywhere near where he'd kept Kaylee. Because that's one of his camps, one of his favorite places to take his victims. He doesn't want to do anything that would make us search harder in that area. And we've been focusing on public paths, recreation areas, parts of the Glades where he'd have access to new victims. All of that makes sense, given the parameters we had at the time. But based on Mary's time of death, and the fact that she was with Kaylee shortly before she died, I think we need to narrow our grid, go back to where we found Kaylee and start over."

"Because of these so-called camps that she told you about?"

"Partly, yes. We've gone along with the FBI's belief that the killer was moving on with every victim, taking what amounted to Plexiglas coffins with him. But Kaylee said he didn't take the boxes. They remained in the ground. That means he has permanent camps, places he's probably worked on for months, or longer, to set up where he never expected they'd be found, because no one would ever think to go that deep, that far, into the swamp to find them. She said he always had plenty of supplies. I bet he keeps those at the camps as well, hidden somewhere. If he doesn't want to haul a box around, he's not going to haul his supplies around every time he moves either. He's not going to just give all that up. He's got a good thing going."

"If these camps are so good, why move at all?"

Zack shrugged. "Maybe he has to head into populated areas on occasion to replenish his supplies, and he worries about the same people seeing him and maybe wondering where he's going. So he switches it up. I don't know. It could just be his signature, the way he plays his game. Or something else. But one thing I know for sure is that he's a creature of habit. He always goes back to the same places eventually."

Drew rocked back in his chair. "Assuming you're right, then what you're telling me is that this guy is counting on us giving up on our searches, not going far enough, deep enough. And he therefore thinks his camp locations are safe from discovery. Meaning, he might still be out there in the same camp where he was the day you found Kaylee?"

"That's what I'm saying."

"So, if we'd just searched another hour or two

where you found her, you think we'd, what, stumble onto one of the camps?"

Zack shook his head. "Not just a couple more hours. It would have to be deep enough in for him to light a campfire that others wouldn't see. And when Kaylee escaped from the camp, the killer had already taken Mary out of the box. As soon as they were out of sight, Kaylee took off. But I discovered her an hour after sunrise. To her, it probably only seemed like a few hours. There's no way she'd have a good grasp of time as dehydrated and messed up as she was. But in reality, if she escaped right after dark and I found her when the sun was up—"

"She could have been on the run in those woods a lot longer than she realized."

"Exactly. We need to go back and go deeper than we've ever gone out there. We need to start over. We need to—"

Drew raised his hand, stopping him. "Hold it. Your timeline is off. If you assume that Kaylee was several hours from the camp when you found her, then how did her captor kill Mary within an hour or two of when you found Kaylee? The M.E. is confident about time of death, based on insect activity, among other things. That timeline implies the camp was only two hours in."

"We went two hours in. And never found it," Zack reminded him.

"No, we never found it." Drew tapped his fingers on the desk, deep in thought.

"The timeline makes sense if Kaylee's captor took Mary with him after discovering that Kaylee had fled. That would have slowed him down, allowing Kaylee to get as far ahead as she did. But of course he did eventually catch up to her."

"And tied or chained Mary somewhere on the trail, probably gagged her so she couldn't scream, while he went to finish Kaylee off? That's what you're thinking, right?"

"Right. But when Cole and I came along and he decided not to risk a confrontation, he turned back, killed Mary and got away while we were riding along in the ambulance and before we realized there was a reason to get the police searching those woods. And remember, again, about the campfires and flashlights Kaylee mentioned. Light from something like a campfire is visible a long way off in the dark. For him to be that bold, he'd have to have his camps far, far away from anywhere that he'd expect someone to ever be. Which reinforces the idea, again, of the camps being even farther into the Glades than we'd thought."

Drew nodded. "That would explain our lack of success with the searches. But I didn't exactly send a bunch of greenhorns out there. They spent hours combing that area and didn't find anything."

"They went in after a rainstorm, which obliterated any trail that Kaylee or the others might have left. And we all believed that the killer wouldn't have stuck around, or returned, assuming instead that he traveled to new places every time. The idea of established camps didn't cross our minds. So when we found no evidence of anyone passing through, we moved on, getting farther and farther away and searching other areas. I'm thinking now that decision was a mistake. I believe the killer will come back, if he hasn't already, which should give us new clues, a new trail to follow."

Drew held his hands up as if in surrender. "All right, all right. You've raised enough questions to make me agree that searching that initial area again where you found Kaylee makes more sense than searching the outlying areas we've been targeting. Especially if all of this adds up to the killer wanting to keep his established bases."

Zack nodded, relieved that Drew was seeing this the way that he was. It helped reassure him that he wasn't grasping, that it made sense to pull the teams off the other grids. He didn't want to kick himself later for doing that if the killer ended up being in one of the areas they stopped searching.

"There's something else to consider." Zack rested his forearms on the desk. "This isn't related to the search strategy. But it *is* related to the case. Kaylee said the killer usually only came there very early in the morning, or at night. If we assume that he switches back and forth between his camps more as a killer's signature, or routine, than because he's worried that someone has seen him in town getting supplies, then there's another plausible explanation for why he's never at the camps during the day."

Drew's mouth tightened into a hard line. "Our perp probably has a job, a day job. And he works and lives close enough to the camps that he can make it to work on time every day. Our killer is Mr. Upstanding Citizen during the day and psycho killer at night. But we'd already figured that as a possibility."

"True, but we also thought he was moving around more than we now think he is. We figured he might be a truck driver, or a salesman, something that would allow for a larger territory. Now I don't think that's the case. We need to tell Special Agent Willow about the camps, that the killer has a more condensed, established area where he keeps his victims, that he probably has a steady day job. Willow should see if he can get us a new profile."

"He's busy on another case now, but I imagine I can at least talk to him over the phone and see if he can get someone to revisit the profile."

"He sounds like an organized killer to me. He's intelligent, able to blend in as a normal guy at work. We're dealing with someone who either called in sick or took vacation on the day of each of the abductions, and was either late or absent the morning that I found Kaylee."

"All good points. I'll ask Willow whether he thinks we should release the profile to the media once he works it up. If people hear the dates of the three abductions that we know about, and that the guy is probably a hunter or avid outdoorsman to be that familiar with the Glades, with little to no nightlife because he's always too busy with his prey to go out for drinks after work, that might give us some hits."

"It also might give you a huge headache with hundreds of tips that lead nowhere, people ratting out the coworkers they can't stand, just to cause them trouble."

Drew shrugged. "I can't let the fear of false tips guide my decisions. If Willow thinks it's a good idea to publish our theories and an updated profile, we will. I'll hire some temps to man the phones if I have to. I don't want another Mary Watkins happening on my watch. So I'll take any help that I can at this point, even if it means dealing with the crazies over a tip line."

Drew shoved away from his desk and stood. "I hope that Miss Brighton can give us more details to add to the ones you gleaned. A description of the vehicle she was hauled around in would be a great start. Maybe her blindfold wasn't always tight and she caught a glimpse of something, anything, that we can use to figure out the vehicle type."

Zack strode to the office door ahead of Drew. "While you and your guys interview Kaylee, I'll get a fresh map and work up new plans for tomorrow's round of searches. I'll brief the teams when they get back today so we'll be ready to go bright and early. God willing, we'll find Sue Ellen and have our killer in custody by tomorrow afternoon."

Chapter Nine

Several hours later Zack stood in another conference room directing the searchers on the plan of attack for tomorrow morning. He leaned over the table and drew a red square on the large map of the Everglades spread out on top. Inside the square were smaller squares with GPS coordinates and the initials of the team who would search each area, all of the grids much closer to Mystic Glades this time.

Because they were starting over.

"Now that you've each selected your search grid, make sure you stick to that grid so that we cover as much ground as possible. No overlaps."

He studied the mix of law-enforcement personnel and civilians, twenty-two men and women standing around the table, eleven two-person teams, as they wrote down information about their assigned search areas and looked at the map. Most of them he knew from working together over the past few weeks doing these laborious searches, like police veterans Robert Spear and Dennis Howard. Some he'd only met at this meeting, fresh teams that were just now joining the other volunteers to help out, including two Florida Fish and Wildlife Conservation officers, Jasper Carraway and Gene Theroux.

Gene was a friend of Cole's and had worked in conjunction with the Collier County Sheriff's Office on many a search-and-rescue operation over the years. Jasper was a veteran from the Northwest Regional FFW Office in the state's panhandle. He'd taken vacation for the express purpose of driving down here to help. *All* of these men and women had volunteered their personal time to slog through the mosquito-laden, alligator-infested swamp looking for the proverbial needle in a haystack.

"Some of you know the routine already but some of you are new so it bears repeating. We'll all meet in the parking lot at zero nine hundred sharp. From there we'll caravan out to the search grid where some deputies will establish our base of operations, providing us food, water, medical supplies, basically any support we might need. That's the rendezvous point for everyone at day's end. Your shifts end at sundown, which is about nineteen-hundred this time of year. For the civilians among you, that's nine in the morning to about seven at night, with breaks whenever you need them. If we find something promising, we'll mark the spot and head straight there the next day using four-wheelers to save time. Then we'll continue the search from where we left off. I know a lot of you are anxious to help, and get frustrated that we're so strict about the cutoff times. But it's too dangerous out there to be fumbling around in the dark. And each of you has to check in at the base so we know that everyone is safe and accounted for."

He looked around, making sure everyone was paying attention. "My usual speech still applies—don't count on your cell phones or even the GPS in your cars to do much good out there. Something about that swamp plays havoc with electronics. Tomorrow morning we're searching an area we searched previously, between five and ten miles northeast of a town called Mystic Glades, depending upon which grid you chose. So some of you on the far side might actually have better luck with your cell phones. But don't rely on that. Memorize the landmarks we've noted on the map to help keep from getting lost. If you find anything that you think could be a clue about Miss Fullerton's whereabouts, or her abductor, or if you just get turned around and lost, stay put, fire a flare, wait for backup."

"Wait," one of them said. "Why are we going over the same search area if we've already checked it out?"

"Because new evidence has surfaced to make us believe that a fresh look at these areas is warranted. Those of you in law enforcement, wear your vests. The rest of you, we'll pass out vests in the morning. I know it's hot and muggy out there and Kevlar can be miserable this time of year. But it might also save your life. So keep it on. We believe the killer may have returned to this section of the Glades, so everyone needs to be on high alert and extra careful."

Surprised glances were exchanged around the table, and the low buzz of conversation filled the room as they considered this new development. Zack made a point of looking at each one of them until he regained their undivided attention. Even though he was just a police chief without any of his own deputies yet—having canceled the interviews the day he found Kaylee—he'd been trusted with the role as the search coordinator. And he took that role very seriously. He didn't want to have anyone hurt or lost on his watch.

"Above all," he continued, "be alert for predators of both the two-foot and four-foot variety. The gators will pretty much leave you alone as long as you leave them alone. But if you end up stepping on one, you're likely to get your leg bitten off. So don't put your foot somewhere that you can't see the bottom. Meaning, stay out of the water, ladies and gentlemen. We're doing a dry-land search. If we decide it's warranted, we'll have teams who specialize in water searches finish up our grids the next day."

"How do we know if it's warranted?" That question came from one of the newer deputies, Rick Carlson. Even though he was a rookie, in his first year on the force, he wasn't some greenhorn kid that Zack had to worry about. This was Carlson's second career after being laid off from his previous job. And he'd been one of the first to volunteer to help with the search.

Everyone, from newbie to seasoned officer, was pulling together like a big family in an effort to locate Fullerton. Zack just hoped he'd be lucky enough to find some deputies half as dedicated as them when he was able to return to the chore of hiring his own employees.

"Each of you is the one who makes that decision," Zack said, in answer to Carlson's question. "After your shift is over tomorrow and you check in at the base of operations, you'll fill out a report showing what grid you searched, along with your recommendations for any further searching of that area. Recommendations include things like footprints, drag marks, bent or broken branches leading to the water... pretty much anything that might indicate that someone went through there into the water.

"In the shallow areas, be on the lookout for fabric or discarded items like canteens, trash of any kind. We're not going into a common camping area so trash would be a dead giveaway that someone's been out there who shouldn't have been. Note those things clearly in your notebooks and then later in your reports. I'll evaluate those reports and decide if other resources and search teams should be brought in to finish up the grids."

Carlson nodded.

"Sounds good." This from Carlson's search partner, Deputy Alan Thomas. Like the rookie, Thomas was fairly new to the force. But unlike Carlson, he had a dozen years of policing underneath his belt, having transferred from Broward County. An avid outdoorsman, he'd grown up in the area, claimed to know the Everglades better than anyone else. And he was itching to find the man who'd dared to use his sacred Glades as his own personal torture chamber for three women.

"Thank you again for volunteering," Zack said. "I'll see you all in the morning."

The teams filed out of the room, leaving Zack to rehang the map on the white board using the magnet circles someone had placed on the upper-right corner. Then he went off to find Deputy Holder, his search partner. They'd been working together for several weeks and he trusted Holder. But after they'd returned from the airport, Holder had disappeared. Zack assumed he'd been sidetracked filling out a report or perhaps doing a favor for one of his teammates. But he was surprised that Holder hadn't at least attended the end-of-day debriefing and planning session like he usually did. Zack was counting on Holder to be his search partner tomorrow. He'd personally chosen the most important grid on the map—the one that encompassed the exact spot where Kaylee had stumbled out onto the road in front of his truck.

He headed down the back hallway, past several other conference rooms on his way to the squad room again. As he passed the room where he'd been with Kaylee earlier, he couldn't help stopping to check on her. He leaned against the wall, several feet back from the large glass cutout.

Sitting at the middle of the table, Kaylee was surrounded by five detectives, including Cole. The FBI had left a week ago, leaving the search to Collier County. They were still engaged in the investigation long-distance, and had offered to put a rush on processing any forensic evidence that might be found. But for the most part they'd gone on to other, higher-profile cases with a better chance of success.

Still, Special Agent Willow would probably spit nails once he found out that he'd missed his chance to interview Kaylee. He'd believed she would be the key to the investigation all along. And from seeing the determined look on Kaylee's face right now as she answered questions, Zack was inclined to agree.

She'd been in that room for hours. Judging by the piles of fast-food trash on the far end of the table, she hadn't even gotten to leave for lunch. But she seemed to be holding up well, so Zack continued down the hallway. At the sound of a door closing, and footsteps behind him, he looked back to see Cole coming out of the conference room where Kaylee had been and heading his way.

"Hold up, Zack." Cole hurried toward him and they stopped and faced each other. "Where are you headed?"

Zack waved toward the end of the hallway that led into the open squad room. "Trying to find Deputy Holder so I can prep him about our search plans for tomorrow. Have you seen him?"

"He got a call from his kid's school. His youngest son is sick so he took off to pick him up and take him to the doctor before they close."

"Anything serious?"

"I don't think so. But the kid was running a fever and the school won't let him come back without a doctor's note."

Zack nodded. Since Jo Lynne's cancer had canceled his plans to be a husband and eventually a father, he wasn't fortunate enough to have any kids himself. But he had enough friends with kids to know the routine. "Guess I'll have to reassign one of the other search teams to join me in the morning."

"Before you go, I wanted to catch you up on the interview with Kaylee," Cole said. "She's remembered an amazing amount of information. She's even worked with a sketch artist to give us a rendering of her abductor."

"I thought he wore a mask the whole time."

"He did, but the artist was able to help her remember other details that could be helpful—like that he's about six feet tall, broad-shouldered, muscular. He's Caucasian with dark eyes, probably brown. From his build and general mannerisms, she guessed him to be anywhere from his late twenties to late thirties."

Zack snorted. "Which means he could be at least half of the men in this building, including me if I wore brown contacts. I thought you said she'd given you an amazing amount of information."

"She did, mostly about his routine, how often he was there." His eyes took on a haunted look. "What he did to her. I've seen a lot over the years, but what she went through is just…beyond horrible. The only good thing is that she was never *successfully* sexually assaulted, if you get my meaning. But she was still assaulted nonetheless. He just couldn't penetrate because of whatever problems he has in that area. He blamed her and punished her for it, thus the cuts, the burns, the bruises." He shook his head. "It's a miracle she survived as long as she did and didn't end up suffering a complete breakdown. She—"

While Cole continued to talk about the interview, Zack tried to tune out the parts about what Kaylee had suffered. The idea that someone could willingly hurt her was beyond his comprehension, and had him fighting mad. It also had him wanting to rush back to the conference room and pull her into his arms, which was beyond stupid. She might have latched on to him as the man she felt had saved her, but that was all she felt for him.

This odd sense of protectiveness that he felt toward her was something he needed to deal with and get past. She'd been through too much to ever want anything more from him than his protection—in spite of how his own thoughts had been turning since picking her up at the airport.

It shamed him to admit it, but seeing her somewhere other than a hospital for a change had him noticing her as the beautiful woman she was and not as a victim anymore. And that had sent a jolt of lust straight to his belly. Which of course made him disgusted with himself for even thinking of her that way. She'd been through unthinkable trauma at the hands of a stranger. She shouldn't have to worry that the man that she thought of as her protector had more than protective feelings for her.

"Which leads me to my next question," Cole said. "Will you do it?"

Zack stared at him, trying to think back to what Cole had been saying.

"Did you hear *anything* I just said?" Cole asked, sounding exasperated.

"Some of it. Sorry. My mind wandered. What did you want me to do?"

The door to the conference room opened down the hall again and Kaylee stepped out, along with her contingent of detectives. She saw him and immediately started his way.

"What's going on?" Zack asked, wishing he'd paid more attention. Because he had a very bad feeling about whatever Cole was expecting of him, and why Kaylee and the others had just stopped beside him, looking at him expectantly.

"Give us a second." Cole pulled Zack several feet away and leaned in close. "You and I both know the investigation has stalled. The only commonality that we've found between the victims, aside from gender and that they were each vacationing alone, is that they all booked their trips through a travel agency. But none of them used the *same* travel agency. We need a break in this case, otherwise I wouldn't—"

"Wait. I hadn't heard that. All three women booked through a travel agency? That's a heck of a coincidence. Do the agencies share some kind of online reservation service? Maybe the killer hacked in and found out the women's itineraries. That's how he was able to surprise them and abduct them."

Cole nodded. "I've already got my team looking into that angle. Even though there isn't an obvious connection between the agencies, we're going to try to get the owners to come in voluntarily for interviews— tonight if we can swing it, or early in the morning. Assuming the owners are cooperative, we'll look at their financials, search for red flags. But it's probably a waste of time, certainly nothing worthy of trying to get a warrant over. At least, so far. We'll see. The problem of course is that even with detectives working the case around the clock, the investigation is slow going, with no truly promising leads. You and I both know that the longer Fullerton is missing, the lower the odds are that we'll find her alive. Which is the only reason I would ever dream of asking you to do this."

Zack narrowed his eyes. "Asking me to do what?"

"Take Kaylee with you to the swamp in the morning, to try to jog her memory."

Zack swore beneath his breath. "There's no way on God's green Earth that I'm taking a victim back out to the scene of the crime. Not this victim, not this crime. She's suffered enough already."

Cole winced. "I know, but she makes a persuasive argument for doing it. She really believes she can lead you to the camp. And if we find that camp, a CSU team can comb it for evidence. A fiber, a fingerprint, could blow the case wide-open and give us a clue that could help us find Fullerton."

"I'm already going back out to search the area where we found Kaylee. So her going with me isn't necessary. If that camp is out there, I'll find it. Without her."

"Like the search team found it the first time?"

He frowned. "We're going deeper this time. And I've checked the weather forecast for tomorrow. Sunny, clear, no problem with it washing out the area and making it impassable. Plus, this time I'll be leading the team in that grid. I was born with a hunting rifle in my hand. I was tracking deer through the woods from the time I could walk. If there are any clues out there to find, I'll find them. But not if I'm slowed down by having to keep an eye on Kaylee the whole time."

Cole glanced back at the others who were watching them and then pulled him a few more feet down the hallway.

"Look, Zack." He kept his voice low. "I understand that you don't want to do this. But I already spoke to the lieutenant and he's on board. We're out of time. I know it. You know it. And Kaylee swears that if we don't take her out there, she'll go by herself."

"Yeah, she made that threat to me earlier, too. We'll just put her in protective custody."

Cole shook his head. "Can't, not against her will. The circumstances don't warrant it unless we had a suspect we were pursuing and a case ready to prosecute— which we don't. So it's our duty to make sure that she's protected when she goes out there, which means assigning her to one of the search teams—yours."

Zack swore and narrowed his eyes at Kaylee as she watched from several feet away. It was obvious that she knew they were discussing her, because her spine stiffened. But she didn't look away or back down. Instead, she returned his stare and crossed her arms over her chest, letting him know that she had no intention of changing her mind.

"She also said that if I didn't agree to her terms that she would tell the media that we didn't let the only witness help with the investigation," Cole said.

Zack immediately shook his head. "I don't think she'd do that. She wouldn't want Mary's family to hear that and get upset."

"Yeah, honestly, I don't see her doing that either.

She wouldn't want to hurt anyone. But she sounded fairly desperate on the phone. That media thing was thrown in at the end because she didn't think I'd cave otherwise."

"Her ploy may have worked on you. But that doesn't mean that I have to play along," Zack said.

"She went through hell out there. She wants to help. Can you really blame me for giving in?"

Zack understood the position Cole was in. And of course he understood wanting to help Kaylee. But this? How could this be called helping?

Cole put his hand on Zack's shoulder, capturing his attention again. "She *is* going out there. And she needs to be with someone who will protect her, someone she trusts. We both know who that is. The psychologist told us in the hospital that Kaylee had bonded to you because you found her, you rescued her. And we brought that same psychologist to the conference room earlier today. Believe it or not, the doctor thinks it's a good idea for Kaylee to revisit the scene, to face her fears basically, and she agrees that if anyone is going to take Kaylee out there, it has to be you."

"You need to fire the psychologist," Zack growled.

Cole simply stared at him, waiting.

Zack blew out a frustrated breath. "This is so messed up."

"I know."

The regret in Cole's voice sounded genuine. Zack

realized that his friend didn't like the idea any more than he did.

He looked over Cole's shoulder at her. And from the hopeful, determined look on her face, he knew she wasn't bluffing about going it alone.

"All right. I'll do it."

He expected Cole to thank him, or at the very least tease him because he'd been able to badger him into agreeing to do what Zack absolutely did *not* want to do. Instead, Cole gave him an uncomfortable look. Like there was something else they needed to discuss, something Zack already knew he wasn't going to be happy about.

"What?" he demanded. "Spit it out. Whatever it is can't be half as bad as what you've already asked."

Cole sighed deeply. "I told you that Kaylee had shared a lot of information. That information came at a price, a bargain she made me agree to at the outset of the interview."

"That I'd take her out to the swamp?"

"Yes."

"And you just assumed that you'd be able to get me to agree."

Cole shrugged. "I wasn't sure, to be honest."

Zack shook his head. "Go on. Finish it. What else did you promise her?"

The words rushed out of Cole like a confession, so quickly that it took them a moment to sink in. When they did, Zack stared at him, dumbfounded. Because what Cole had just asked him wasn't *half* as bad as his first request.

It was worse.

Chapter Ten

As hotels went, Kaylee was used to far more luxurious accommodations than what this one offered. But since the La Quinta was less than two miles from the sheriff's office, where the search parties would rendezvous in the morning, this was the perfect location. Not that she'd had a choice. Zack refused to let a victim pay the tab, so he chose a place that was police-budget friendly. There was a Red Roof Inn a little closer to the sheriff's office. But it didn't have inside hallways or what he called good vantage points, whatever that meant. So, the La Quinta it was.

But it wasn't the lack of luxuries, or even the fact that the suites had been sold out, leaving them sharing a room with double beds, that had her nervous as Zack slid the hotel key card into the electronic lock. It was the tight, shuttered expression on his face as he held the door open for her to enter.

The kind, caring man she'd met nearly a month ago had dissolved the instant that Cole told him her deal—that she would only cooperate in the investigation if Zack was assigned to her—meaning, where she went, he went, including to a hotel for the night.

He'd taken her to Marco's Bar & Grill for dinner after leaving the sheriff's office, where they'd eaten a rather delicious seafood dinner that she'd have enjoyed any other time. But sitting in silence with Zack's stoic profile across from her as he monitored every person coming in and out of the restaurant took all the pleasure out of the meal. She'd been more than relieved to get out of there. But it didn't look like the evening was improving now that they were at the hotel.

She smiled thinly at Zack as she swept inside, not that it mattered. He was cold, stony, remote—polite, but not doing anything that could be misconstrued as friendly either. She tried not to let it bother her, but it was as if her only support net had been ripped away. The one person who seemed to understand her, whom she'd felt a kinship with, was now treating her like a stranger. And it hurt.

Keeping her expression devoid of emotion, she surveyed her surroundings—which took only a few seconds. The short hallway led past a small bathroom and into the bedroom. A dresser, work desk and TV took up the wall on the right. The two beds, separated by an end table, were on the left. Filmy white curtains framed a large window at the end of the room, with an air-conditioning unit beneath it, currently set to arctic levels. The room was freezing.

She shivered and rubbed her bare arms as she considered which bed to choose. Zack took the choice away from her, plopping the duffel bag he'd brought from his truck down onto the bed closest to the door, and placing her small suitcase on the bed nearest the window.

He'd insisted on a second-floor room when he'd registered. In answer to her question of why, he'd mumbled something about controlling access points. He made a quick circuit of the room, checking the window, pulling the heavy drapes over the small flimsy ones, blocking out the rather unimpressive view of the parking lot. Then he adjusted the air-conditioner and grabbed a thermal blanket out of the closet, tossing it onto the foot of her bed as he passed back to the main door.

Maybe he was paying more attention to her than she'd thought. She nodded her gratitude and wrapped the blanket around her shoulders. He checked the lock on the door, threw the security bar across it and surprised her by tilting the desk chair underneath the door handle, as well. Was he normally that careful or was he doing that just to make her feel secure? She didn't know, didn't ask.

Without a word, he grabbed a small leather toiletry bag from his duffel, went into the bathroom and firmly shut the door behind him.

Kaylee sighed and unzipped her suitcase. Might as well get ready for bed. Tomorrow was going to be a difficult day, probably the most difficult she'd faced since escaping the devil. And she'd need a good night's sleep to ensure that she was as ready as she could be, and hopefully, ready to piece all of her memories together and find the camp where she'd been held.

After taking her own turn in the bathroom, she slid into bed.

A whisper of sound had her eyes fluttering open. She frowned at the unfamiliar ceiling above her for a moment before remembering where she was—the hotel room. A soft, yellow glow of light dimly lit the room. She turned her head on her pillow, saw that the bedside clock said it was just a little after midnight. But she didn't even remember falling asleep. And the bed beside hers was empty.

She gasped with alarm and sat up, clutching her covers to her chest. Relief swept through her when she saw Zack. He hadn't left her, as her sleepy mind had at first assumed. He was sitting at the desk at the foot of her bed, writing something on a piece of paper. While she watched, he reached back without turning around and gently patted her leg, all while whispering, "Shhh, it's okay, Kaylee. It's okay. You're safe. Shhh."

When she didn't move or say anything, the patting eventually stopped. He pulled his hand back then smoothed out what she now realized was some kind of map. She had a very bad feeling about why he'd patted her by rote, without even turning to look at her, and why he was awake at this hour.

Testing her theory, she gasped again. Immediately, his arm shot out and he started patting her again, whispering those nonsensical words, without turning around.

Shame washed over her. Obviously, she must have had one of her awful nightmares. And Zack had soothed her, helped chase the nightmare away. But, as often happened, the nightmare had returned. And now he'd, what, given up on sleeping? He was working and keeping an ear out for her distress so he could chase her nightmares away every time they came back?

She wrapped her arms around her waist and scooted back against the headboard. The movement was significant enough to make him turn his head this time, and his eyes widened when he saw that she was awake.

"You okay?" His voice was somber, quiet, and... tired. There were dark circles under his eyes.

"I'm sorry," she said. "What did I do? Scream?"

He hesitated, watching her, almost warily. "Once."

"So you soothed me in my sleep, got me to quiet down. And then I kept slipping back into my nightmare." She waved toward his hand resting on the foot of the bed. "I ruined your sleep. You've been sitting there for, what, hours? Calming me down every time

I grow restless again. I'm so, so sorry. Why didn't you just wake me up?"

He pulled his hand back from the bed. "I couldn't sleep, anyway, not your fault. No reason for both of us to be tired in the morning."

She let out a sigh and watched him. He wasn't wearing a shirt, so she let her gaze idly slip across his golden-tanned skin, his sculpted shoulders and muscular arms. Biting her lower lip, she allowed her gaze to slide lower, tracing down to see that he was wearing shorts, but nothing else except a pair of white ankle socks. The man was practically naked, and it was doing all kinds of crazy things to her belly, not to mention the room suddenly seemed to have heated at least ten degrees.

"I'll try to be more quiet," he said, causing her gaze to rise to his face.

As if he was suddenly aware of her fascination with his near-naked state, he frowned and turned back around.

The sound that had awakened her, that whisper of noise, sounded again. Curious, and completely awake now, she tossed the covers back and slid her own sock-covered feet out of bed. She wasn't one for walking on hotel carpet in bare feet, not wanting to risk trodding without shoes where countless others had been. She wondered if he wore socks to keep his feet warm, or whether he was a bit of a germophobe like her.

Since she was wearing long-sleeved and long-legged pale yellow pajamas, and a bra for modesty, she didn't bother grabbing her robe. She padded across the floor to stand beside him. Since the only true desk chair was currently propped under the handle to the main door, he'd pulled one of the two small armchairs over and was sitting in that. She grabbed the other one and pulled it beside his and then plopped down.

He frowned at her but then went back to his perusal of the map.

She took the opportunity to study his chiseled profile, admire the thick lashes that framed his dark blue eyes.

His frown deepened and he blew out an impatient breath as if he was aware of her perusal. "Did you need something?"

"Just...wondering what you're doing."

He sighed again, obviously not thrilled that she'd joined him. But she'd already discovered that he was too polite to be out-and-out rude or mean-spirited in any way, so he didn't tell her to go away. Plus, she knew something else about him now. He cared, really cared. A man who didn't care wouldn't have gone to the trouble of moving himself to the foot of her bed where he could calm her through her nightmares. A man who didn't care would have simply woken her up then tried to get his own sleep while she was the one sitting up and worrying that she might fall asleep again and cry out.

No, Zack wasn't the angry man he'd been since they'd left the sheriff's office. That Zack was the exception, not the rule. The real Zack was the one that had saved her from the devil, the one who'd seemed aggravated at first at the airport, but who'd quickly exchanged that aggravation for concern when he'd realized how freaked out she was about being caught in such a public, busy place. That was the Zack she was most comfortable with, the man she admired. So this one, the irritable one, didn't bother her anymore.

"Why are you looking at a map?" she asked, since he hadn't answered her.

One second went by, two.

"I'm reviewing the topography of the grid we'll be searching tomorrow." The tone of his voice sounded more resigned now, less angry, as if he'd realized she wasn't going back to sleep unless he answered her questions, and he didn't see the point in arguing.

She leaned toward him, automatically clutching his shoulder for balance as she peered at the map. "Why?"

His gaze shot to her hand. But he didn't say anything, didn't ask her to move it, so she didn't. She simply looked up at him and smiled.

His eyes widened and he looked away, his Adam's apple bobbing in his throat. She was making him nervous. And she was enjoying it. He'd made her nervous and upset since the moment Cole had ordered him to watch over her for the night and take her to the search sight tomorrow. Served him right that she was returning the favor now.

He cleared his throat. "I'm memorizing as much of it as I can, checking out the terrain, where the canals go, its general location in relation to the highway." He looked at her again, his emotions shuttered away, once again the calm, in-control police officer. "Cell phones, GPS trackers, even compasses are temperamental out there. Your safety is my responsibility and I don't want to get you lost."

Staring into those beautiful blue eyes, that achingly handsome face, up this close, with him half-naked and her in her pajamas in a hotel room no less, at any other time, would have made her giddy with the rush of hormones and the beginnings of a raging crush. But after everything she'd gone through, none of those emotions seemed appropriate. Instead, they were ridiculous, wrong. So why, then, was her skin flushing hot, her gaze dropping to his lips?

"Kaylee." His voice sounded tight, strained. "What are you doing?"

She frowned then looked down and realized she was stroking his naked shoulder. If her face had seemed hot before, now it positively burned…with embarrassment. She jerked her hand back and leaned away from him.

"Sorry," she murmured. She closed her eyes and

shook her head. "Seriously. I'm really, really sorry. I can't believe I did that."

"Why don't you get back in bed, go to sleep?" he said. "It's going to be a trying day tomorrow, a long day."

"What about you?" She waved toward the map. "You need your sleep, too."

Something dark, angry flickered in the depths of his eyes. "You didn't seem worried about that when you blackmailed Cole into convincing me to take you here tonight."

She jerked back. "Why are you so mad about that?"

"I don't like being forced to do something I don't want to do."

"What's the real reason?"

"Excuse me?"

She rolled her eyes. "Come on. You're a big, strong, smart man. You don't work for Cole, or even Lieutenant Shlafer. You're working as a volunteer, because I was discovered in your territory, your jurisdiction. I don't believe for one second that you resent me for blackmailing you. Because if you really didn't want to look after me, you'd have simply said no and walked away. So what's the real reason that you're so upset?"

His eyes darkened, and she could tell she'd struck some kind of chord in him. But what? She really didn't understand why he was so angry.

"I don't want you in danger," he finally said. "The

lieutenant never should have agreed to let you go back to the swamp."

She cocked her head, studying him. "I don't want to go either, Zack. But what kind of person would I be if I don't?"

She watched him for another moment, and then she sucked in a breath as a thought occurred to her. "I'm sorry. I didn't even consider… I never asked whether this, staying in the hotel room together, could be a problem for you. Is there a girlfriend or fiancée who might be upset about you staying with me? I'm sorry that I didn't think about that before. I should have asked."

The blood seemed to drain from his face, and she belatedly realized she'd said something that had hurt him, perhaps crossed a line. What had she said? Girlfriend? Fiancée? Why would that make him act like she'd physically struck him?

And then she knew.

Because she'd felt like that once herself, that devastating feeling of loss when, back in middle school, her best friend was killed in a car accident. Without thinking about it, she took his left hand in both of hers.

"I'm so sorry," she whispered. "How did she die?"

He froze, shocked. "How did you know?"

"Pain recognizes pain, I suppose. I was in eighth grade when I lost my best friend in an accident. I still remember how I felt, how I still feel when something happens to make me think about her. Your loss is more recent, I would guess?"

"Five years. We were college sweethearts, engaged to be married. She felt a lump one day. Four months later she was gone."

"Breast cancer?"

He nodded.

"I'm so sorry. What was her name?"

He didn't look like he wanted to tell her, but then he did.

"Jo Lynne."

Kaylee had always been what her mom called a touchy-feely kind of person, sometimes crossing boundaries, getting into other people's space without realizing it. She couldn't help it. If she felt bad for someone, she wanted to make them feel better. And since hugging made her feel better, she didn't stop to think about her next action. She just slid her arms around Zack's waist and rested her head against his chest, hugging him close.

At first he didn't move, just stiffened in his chair with her awkwardly leaning against him. But then it was like a dam broke inside him, and he was holding her just as tightly as she was holding him. His cheek nestled against the top of her head, his soft breath fanning out against her scalp. With her encouraging him, he began to tell her about Jo Lynne—slowly at first, then the words rushed out, in ebbs and flows, as he told her about this woman he'd once loved enough to plan forever with her.

Until he lost her.

When he stopped talking, they continued to hold each other for a long time. Her ear pressed against his chest, listening to the strong, steady beat of his heart. Him gently rubbing her back, his cheek moving every once in a while against the top of her head. When he finally pulled away and stared down at her, she expected to see regret, perhaps even embarrassment that he'd confessed his pain to her, a woman he probably thought of as a relative stranger, even though she felt like she knew him better than most men she'd ever met. But there was no embarrassment, no regret, no anger anymore. There was something else in the depths of his eyes. Relief, perhaps? That he'd finally been able to talk about something that she sensed he'd never really spoken about before?

His hand shook as he feathered her hair back from her face. He swallowed, hard, and then he was gone, shutting the bathroom door between them, as if he needed that barrier to compose himself again.

She folded up his map, set the chairs back where they belonged then slid into her bed, leaving only the dim light on as she waited.

A few minutes later he padded into the room, looked down at her, his expression solemn. Then, without a word, he flicked off the light.

The room was plunged into total darkness. She

hated the dark, always slept with a light on. But the familiar, smothering fear that she expected didn't come. Instead, she felt…safe. And now that Zack didn't seem angry at her anymore, the tension in the room was gone and she knew even before she closed her eyes that this time the nightmares wouldn't come. This time she'd be able to sleep until morning, without fear.

Covers shifted as he moved in his bed just a few feet away.

"Kaylee?" His deep voice broke the quiet.

"Hmm?"

"I was angry about having to spend the night in a hotel room with you, because since meeting you, for the first time in five years, I thought about another woman besides Jo Lynne. *Really* thought about her, about *you*. Do you understand?"

She smiled in the dark. "I understand. Zack?"

"Yes?"

"I care about you, too. And I wouldn't mind seeing you sometime…after this is all over. That is, if you want to."

His breath shuddered out of him. "I want."

The tension that had evaporated earlier was suddenly so thick she could barely breathe. For a moment she wondered what, if anything, she should do. Part of her wanted to join him in his bed. But it would be a mistake. She was too damaged, still fighting nightmares, still trying to overcome what had happened to her. This…this attraction she felt for Zack, even though it was mutual, was too new to act on. The timing was completely wrong, and she suspected they both knew it.

"Good night, Kaylee."

His covers rustled again and she sensed that he'd turned over, facing away from her. Decision made— he'd made it for both of them.

She let out a breath that was equal parts relief and disappointment. "Good night, Zack."

Chapter Eleven

Zack pulled his truck into the parking lot of the sheriff's office, with Kaylee sitting tense at his side, clutching her hands together so tightly that her knuckles had turned white. No doubt she was worried about visiting the search site, but no more worried than he was. That worry had kept him tossing and turning at the hotel last night. But he'd finally managed to fall asleep. But then Kaylee's frightened sobs had awakened him. He'd grabbed his gun from beneath his pillow and bolted upright in one smooth motion, sweeping the pistol back and forth, seeking out whatever had scared her. Then she'd thrashed and moaned again, and he'd realized there weren't any bad guys hiding in the shadows of their hotel room. The bad guys were hiding in the shadowed recesses of her mind.

His heart had clenched in his chest at how terrified and pale she looked in the glow of the bedside clock as the nightmare gripped her. So he'd put his gun away and leaned over, ready to shake her awake.

But the moment he'd whispered her name and placed his hand on her shoulder, she'd calmed and rolled over to face him with a smile, still asleep.

He'd pulled his hand back and studied her quiet beauty, watching her expression to make sure the nightmare was really gone. She really was a striking woman. Just remembering those long, shapely legs and firm, high breasts that were beneath the covers had his own breath hitching, his pulse slamming. And just like every time he thought of her *that* way, guilt crushed down upon him and he berated himself for a fool.

And then she'd cried out in her sleep.

Once again he patted her shoulder, whispered soothing words. And once again she'd settled into a peaceful sleep. After the third time, he'd given up on trying to sleep himself and had figured he might as well get some work done—thus how he'd ended up at the desk, reaching over to pat her and whisper to her every time the nightmares came back.

And wishing desperately that he'd stuck to his guns when he'd first told Cole that he wasn't going to a hotel with Kaylee.

Of course Cole had no way of knowing just how attracted to Kaylee Zack was, and not just because of her looks either. Although stunning, especially with most of the bruises healed, there were plenty of other beautiful women that Zack had seen or known. Her looks were only part of her appeal. What called out to him was their intense shared history right after the accident, the days spent holding her hand, sitting by her hospital bed. The bond they'd formed was a strong one, and not one-sided at all the way her head doctor had assumed. He felt just as connected to her as she did to him.

And he didn't know what in the world to do about it.

Wanting Kaylee was a dead end. She'd been through too much and needed more time to heal. And even though she'd surprised him at the hotel with her flirtatiousness, he took it for what it must be—her acting out, being silly, to cut the tension between them. It certainly couldn't be real, not after what she'd suffered.

She was strong, tough, and he admired her for that. But even someone as courageous and determined as she was couldn't possibly be ready to get back to "real" life so quickly after what she'd gone through. And he'd do good to remember that. His job today was clear—keep her alive, unhurt. Then he'd turn her over to Cole and be on his way, letting Kaylee get back to her life while he returned to his.

"Zack?"

He blinked and realized he must have been staring at Kaylee, because she was looking at him uncertainly, waving a hand in front of his face. His face heated and he turned the engine off.

"Looks like we're the first search team here." He

gestured toward the near-empty parking lot. "We can have a cup of coffee inside the break room while we wait."

She gave him a quizzical look, but hopped out of the truck as he came around to her side. They headed into the building down the same long hallway that she'd been in yesterday. But as soon as they started to pass the conference room with the big glass window, she stopped so fast that the soles of her all-weather hiking boots squeaked against the floor.

Zack was immediately on alert, stepping half in front of her, hand automatically on the butt of his holstered pistol as he looked to see what had startled her. But all he saw was Cole and another detective sitting with their backs to the window, questioning a thin, blonde-haired woman who looked no more threatening than the average housewife. But as he glanced at Kaylee, he realized she wasn't scared; she was just startled, and more than a little confused.

"Why is Sandy in there?" she asked, as if he should know.

He shrugged. "I've never seen her before. Who is she?"

"Sandy Gonzalez. She's a long-time friend of my family, and also the owner of the travel agency that I used to schedule my trip and my flight down here yesterday. She lives in Miami. I wonder if something has happened. She must have come to see me."

She headed toward the door.

"Hold it." Zack stopped her just as she started to turn the knob, and he gently pulled her back. "Looks fairly intense in there. I don't think we should interrupt their meeting."

But Sandy was already staring at Kaylee through the window, her eyes wide with surprise.

Kaylee raised a hand in greeting, but instead of waving back, Sandy's face turned a bright red and she looked away.

Kaylee slowly lowered her hand and looked up at Zack. "What's going on? She looks...scared."

He wasn't sure he agreed with that assessment. If anything, she looked guilty to him. But guilty of what? That was the real question.

"You said she booked your trip. Did you always use a travel agent for trips here in the state, even though you live in Florida?"

"Actually, no. I mostly used her agency when I planned a trip out of state. Let's face it, it's only a few hours from here to Miami. I could easily set up my own tours and hotels for that. But she called me, asked where I was planning on vacationing this year and said she had a great deal for a tour package in the Everglades." She shrugged. "I thought it sounded fun so I went ahead."

"She called you? Why would she do that?"

"Because I hadn't called her yet. I take a week's vacation every July, and most of the time I call her to help me schedule it. I guess since I hadn't called yet, she decided to call me."

"Has she ever done that before? Called you first?"

She shook her head and stared through the window at the woman who was still avoiding looking at her. "Actually, no. But she didn't want me to miss out on the deal. Poor Sandy. She feels terrible about what happened." She frowned. "I just can't imagine why she's here."

Zack could imagine exactly why she was there. And he didn't feel sorry for the woman one bit. In fact, he'd like to strangle her about now. Because he remembered that Cole had told him yesterday that all three of the women that they believed were taken by *the devil* had booked their trips through travel agencies. And knowing that Miss Gonzalez's agency was based in Miami, he felt it was a safe bet that she wouldn't have driven or flown all the way to the opposite coast this early in the morning unless there was a darn good reason—like that the police wanted to interrogate her. And he didn't see Cole wasting time with the logistics of getting Gonzalez here in person unless he had a compelling reason for it.

Although Zack had told Kaylee to wait, he no longer felt the compulsion to do so himself. He wanted to know what was going on, exactly how it related to their current case and why Gonzalez had broken protocol by calling Kaylee to offer her a trip instead of the other way around.

He rapped on the glass. Cole looked over his shoulder and nodded. After saying something to the detective on his right, he shoved his chair back and headed out of the room. After closing the door behind him, he motioned for them both to follow him down the hall.

After a quick knock on another door to make sure no one was inside, he ushered them into a small conference room. All this one boasted was a round table with four chairs. Not a snack machine or window in sight.

Zack pulled one of the chairs out for Kaylee, who murmured her thanks as she sat. Then he took the chair to her right across from Cole.

"Spill," Zack said. "What's the connection between the travel agencies and our case?"

Cole's brows rose. "You don't waste any time, do you?"

"Don't have time to waste. The search parties will be here soon and we'll have to head out."

Cole greeted Kaylee before looking at Zack again. "Obviously, Kaylee must have told you that woman is Sandy Gonzalez, owner of Aventuras Travel Agency based out of Miami. What we didn't know until late last night after digging through layer after layer of shell companies is that she's also the owner of several other travel agencies around the state. Want to guess who owns the agencies that Mary and Sue Ellen used?"

"Sandy Gonzalez," Zack said.

"Bingo."

Kaylee glanced from Zack to Cole. "Wait, you're saying she hid the fact that she owned the other agencies? Shell companies are fake companies, right?"

"More or less," Cole said. "They're real on paper, legal entities. Mostly, people use them to hide true ownership, not necessarily for illegal purposes. Sometimes it just has to do with marketing, like a gas and oil company not wanting people to know they also own, say, a milk plant—because gas, oil and food don't exactly sound appetizing together. No harm in using shell companies to keep the image of the different entities intact and separate. But other people use them to hide income, or for other illegal purposes. In this case, there's nothing illegal about how Miss Gonzalez set up her companies. But that doesn't mean that she didn't do something illegal."

Again, Kaylee glanced back and forth between them. Zack could tell by the wary look on her face that she didn't need to know about shell companies to see that something wasn't right. But she also didn't want to believe that her friend had done anything wrong.

"Okay," she said. "I don't have to be a detective to think that sounds like a big coincidence. But it has to be, right? What other explanation could there be?" When neither of them spoke, she frowned. "You can't think she had something to do with my abduction. That's preposterous. She wouldn't do that."

Cole shrugged. "I think it's a possibility, yes."

She laughed then sobered. "You're serious?" At his nod, she said, "The person who abducted me, who assaulted me, tortured me, was definitely a man. I may not be able to describe his face, but I have no doubt whatsoever that my attacker was male. So what's your theory here? How could she possibly be involved?"

Zack eyed Cole. "Good question. What would she have to gain by arranging the abductions, if that's what you think happened?"

Kaylee sucked in a startled breath.

"I haven't figured that out yet," Cole said. "But we've only been questioning her for about a half hour. My team just got a judge to sign off on a subpoena for her financial records about an hour ago. I've got one of my best detectives rousing a bank manager as we speak to try to get some quick info over the phone rather than wait for the usual ad hoc reports that could take days or weeks. We don't have that kind of time if we're going to find Sue Ellen alive."

"Hold it, hold it." Kaylee waved her hands in the air. "Financial records? Subpoena? What do you expect to find? You think she hired someone to kidnap us? There weren't any ransom demands. What would she have to gain?"

She shook her head like she thought Cole was crazy. "Have you seen the publicity she's been getting? In Miami, at least, I can tell you she's been getting a lot, all of it bad. If this cockamamy idea of her somehow being behind the abductions for financial gain were true, trust me, it totally backfired. I heard she's had to lay off half her staff. No one wants to book vacations with an agency whose last client was abducted during the arranged tour and tortured for three months."

"She's right," Zack said. "There doesn't seem to be an obvious financial benefit for Miss Gonzalez to be involved in any way."

"Exactly." Kaylee crossed her arms and sat back in her chair, looking smug and aggravated at the same time. "I can't believe you brought her here to interrogate her like some criminal."

Cole's brows rose again. "If you were in that conference room with her, listening to her avoid most of my questions, I highly doubt you'd feel so confident right now. She's definitely hiding something. I just haven't figured out what that is…yet. But I will."

Zack's cell phone vibrated against his waist and he pulled it out to check the screen. "Looks like the search parties are waiting for us in the parking lot." He put the phone away and they all stood. He eyed Kaylee's determined look. "I don't suppose there's anything at all that I can do to talk you out of going out there with me?"

She immediately shook her head. "Not a chance."

He sighed. "I didn't think so." He held the door open for her. "Let's do this, then. Let's go find Sue Ellen."

Cole walked with them down the hallway, toward

the front lobby and the doors that opened onto the parking lot.

"Who's your search team partner today? Deputy Holder called out this morning, said his wife's sick along with his son. He's staying home to take care of both of them. You're not searching your grid alone, are you? Just you and Miss Brighton?"

Zack gave him a droll look. "You know me better than that. I'm not taking any more chances with Kaylee's safety than absolutely necessary. I sent out a group text this morning from the hotel and got four volunteers to help Kaylee and me search our assigned area. Two of them are your men, Alan Thomas and Rick Carlson."

Cole nodded his approval. "They're both new to the Collier County Sheriff's Office, but I've heard they've been a great team in the searches so far. And even though Carlson's a rookie, Thomas has a dozen years of policing experience from his stint in Broward County. You said four guys, though. Who are the other two?"

"A couple of Florida Fish and Wildlife Conservation officers are going to follow us out there in their vehicle. Gene Theroux is a local veteran, knows this area inside and out. The other FFW guy, Jasper Carraway, drove all the way from the panhandle area a couple of days ago—on vacation, no less—to volunteer his expertise in the search. Between them and your two deputies, we should be good to go."

Relief flashed across Cole's face, and for the first time in days he smiled a genuine smile as he looked at Kaylee. "I've been worried and second-guessing myself ever since I agreed to let you assist us in the search. But Chief Scott's assembled a crack team. You've got nothing to worry about."

"I was never worried," she said. "I know that Zack will keep me safe."

Cole's grin widened. "I'm sure that *Zack* will do just that."

Zack narrowed his eyes in warning, but Cole just laughed and headed back down the hall.

"It looks like everyone is waiting for us." Kaylee motioned toward the search teams milling around outside the glass front doors.

He nodded and held one of the doors open for her. But as they stepped outside, he couldn't help but wonder if he was doing the right thing. Crack team or not, they were about to go into the territory of a killer who knew the swamp better than any of them, and had made it his own personal, sick playground. Zack just hoped that by taking Kaylee there, he wasn't playing right into the killer's hands.

KAYLEE WORKED TO control her breathing as Zack brought his truck to a stop on the same dirt road where he'd rescued her close to a month ago, deep in the Everglades. And behind his truck, another four-by-four pickup pulled to a stop, the one with the two

Fish and Wildlife officers. Kaylee knew she should have hopped right out, started the search, but she couldn't seem to make her hand move to the door handle.

It had been hard enough getting into this truck at the airport, because it reminded her of the swamp and what had happened. But she'd thought she'd gotten past that, and had assured Zack that she was fine taking the truck from the sheriff's office to the Glades, particularly because it was four-wheel drive and they might need that to keep from getting stuck. And she *had* been fine, at first. But then he'd insisted on bringing two deputies with them, two searchers who'd volunteered when Zack asked for backup to make sure she'd be safe when he brought her out here—on the off chance that they happened to stumble onto the killer.

Carlson and Thomas had both greeted her politely enough at the sheriff's office, but she'd instinctively taken a step back when Carlson moved to shake her hand. Thomas raised his brows and didn't even offer a handshake. She'd apologized but still couldn't bring herself to even look them in the eyes.

Something about being surrounded by three tall, muscular men while contemplating getting into a truck to go to the swamp had her feeling claustrophobic and jittery. It made no sense. These were the good guys, especially Zack. But she couldn't shake the feeling of impending doom that had settled over her. And once they were on their way, the closer they'd gotten to the swamp, the tighter her nerves seemed to wind until she was ready to explode.

Thinking about facing her fears and *actually* facing them were two entirely different things. Because, as she sat in the passenger seat now, vaguely aware that the men had gotten out of the truck, as well as the two other men in the truck behind them, all she could do was stare at the bushes and trees lining the road.

She knew those bushes, knew those trees. They were in her nightmares every night when she closed her eyes. And now, seeing them again, the place where she'd run from the devil and out in front of this very truck, she started to shake. A keening sound carried on the wind, like a hurt animal, in terrible pain.

The passenger door opened and suddenly Zack was there, leaning in, saying soothing words. And to her shame, she realized the keening sound was coming from her. She clamped her lips together to stop the noise and focused on the rich timbre of his voice. It was like a physical thing, stroking down her spine, calming her, even though the buzzing in her ears made it impossible for her to make out his words.

His hands, warm, gentle, slid under her palms, carefully pressing up against her hands. She blinked and realized her nails were digging into the dash, and that he was trying to get her to loosen her hold. But he didn't put his hands over hers or try to force her. Instead, he let her be in control, keeping his hands open, under hers, with just the barest of pressure as if to tell her he was there to help her, but that it was up to her to decide if or when to let go.

A rush of unexpected longing swept through her, breaking through her fear. This man was so solid, strong and yet amazingly gentle. He somehow always seemed to know what she needed to help her focus and beat down her panic. If only she could have met him under different circumstances. She had no doubt that they could have been great friends, or perhaps something deeper, special, lasting. But not now. It was too late for her, for them, even if there ever could have been a "them." She was broken. She only had to look at her nails scoring the dash to see just how broken she was.

"We can turn around, go back to the station right now," he was saying, as his words finally penetrated her fog of fear. "It's okay. You've been incredibly brave just getting this far. We can go back and—"

"No." Her voice came out a squeaky croak. She cleared her throat and forced her hands to relax their death-like grip on the dash, and instead slid her hands over his and threaded their fingers together. "I'm ready. I can do this."

His frown told her he wasn't quite so sure, but she didn't let him take the time to think about it. She pulled her hands back and took off her seat belt. He hadn't wanted to take her out here to begin with, and it wouldn't take much for him to turn around and take her back to Naples. She had to do this. Now. Because after today, she never wanted to come back to this godforsaken place again. Ever.

Swinging her legs to the side, she forced him back as she hopped out of the truck. The two deputy searchers stood off to the side of the road, watching her warily, as if they thought she might freak out any minute and start screaming like a crazy woman. The FFW officers stood a few feet farther back, whispering to each other—probably about her.

Kaylee straightened her spine and closed the truck door. "Let's go." She started past Zack, but he put his hands on her shoulders and turned her toward him.

"Are you sure about this?" He kept his voice low so the two men behind them couldn't hear him.

"What you're really asking is whether I'll break down into a blubbering puddle, or curl up in a fetal position, or maybe run around in circles screaming, right?"

His eyes widened, but before he could say anything, she continued. "No. I'm not sure that I can handle this. But I am sure about two things. First, with you beside me, I'm safe. So if I do curl up in a ball, I have every confidence that you'll make sure I get home unhurt."

His lips twitched as if he wanted to smile, but instead he nodded. "Second?"

She looked past the truck to the bushes, to the exact spot where she could still see the devil standing, his evil eyes peeking out through his mask as she lay helpless in the road. "Second, if I don't do this now, I never will. And if I don't do this, I'll never forgive myself." She squared her shoulders and pointed to the spot where she'd last seen the evil man who'd changed her life forever. "That's where I ran out of the woods. That's where we'll start."

Without waiting for him, she started across the road.

Zack directed the FFW officers to head into the trees a short distance away, keeping parallel with them. "Thomas, Carlson, you follow Miss Brighton and me, but keep back about ten feet. Give us some space, but not too much," Zack told the men as he kept pace with her. "I don't want any surprises today."

"Neither do I," she whispered.

"Did you say something?" he asked, staring down at her.

"Nothing." She'd stopped at the edge of the road, right where the devil had stopped, and peered through a break in the trees. Zack stood quietly beside her, waiting, watching her intently.

Without turning from her study of the path, she held out her right hand. Zack immediately took it, his strong, warm fingers holding hers in a solid grip that had her breathing easier.

Zack will protect me. Zack will protect me. She kept repeating the mantra over and over in her mind as she closed her eyes, using his hand as her anchor, allowing the jumbled pieces of her memory to flit around, bouncing against each other, until they began to stick together and form a bigger picture.

"I'm here, Kaylee." Zack's deep voice was reassuring, anchoring her like his hand, keeping the evil at bay. "You're okay."

She nodded, letting him know she heard him, as she tried to fit the pieces together. Without opening her eyes, she said, "When I escaped, I counted every step I took, repeated every turn in my mind, looked for oddly shaped trees, fallen logs, anything I could use to help orient me, so I could find my way back." The pieces of her memories bumped, turned, shifted and then...clicked. She opened her eyes, and like magic, the path opened up before her. "This way." She stepped into the woods.

Chapter Twelve

The devil is in the details.

As Kaylee stepped over a fallen log, she couldn't help thinking that old saying was never more true than it was today. She used to tell herself that mantra when studying for an exam at school, or when filling out financial reports at the bank where she worked or even when planning her annual vacations. Because details mattered to her, had always mattered. It was about doing things right, not making mistakes. And today, remembering each and every detail of her flight from the man who'd abducted and tortured her, the man she'd dubbed the devil, was even more critical than anything else she'd ever done. If she didn't get these details right, someone else might die.

So she took her time, methodically studying every group of trees, every misshapen bush that they passed as she moved deeper and deeper into the woods. It was as if she were outside her own body, looking down from above, trying to map out her escape route—backward. And it was so…incredibly…

difficult. Trying to reverse every step she'd taken, even though she'd noted landmarks, funny-shaped branches, or half-rotten logs as she'd made her escape, she hadn't realized how hard it would be to try to remember those details in reverse to get back to the spot from where she'd once run.

She stopped, let out an exasperated breath and studied the trees around her.

"Take your time," Zack said beside her, his voice, as usual, deep and soothing. "You're doing great. Just relax. Don't try to force it."

She grimaced, remembering the last time she'd tried to force it—at the hospital, when the detectives and FBI agent kept badgering her and badgering her with more and more questions. She'd gone completely blank, and it had taken weeks before she'd been able to remember anything again.

Zack was right. She needed to relax, stop trying to force it. She nodded and closed her eyes, thinking back to nearly a month ago, the last time she'd been in these woods.

"Think about the smells," Zack said. "How did the woods smell that day?"

She frowned up at him. "Smells?"

"Close your eyes again," he urged. When she did, he said, "Scent is one of the strongest triggers for memories. Just picture yourself in the woods that day, but forget about the devil. You're moving through the woods, a traveler, lost, trying to find a way out. What do you hear?"

"Birds. I hear…birds. An owl I think, and some other bird that would chirp, a high-pitched sound, about seven or eight times. Then it would stop and start up again a few seconds later."

"Was the wind blowing?"

She shook her head. "No. It was hot, muggy, like now. Only an occasional breeze."

"What did the air smell like? Was it musty? Wet?"

"Wet. Yes. Like…like the smell of moss on a tree. Or perhaps mud. It was very wet."

"It had rained a lot that week, practically a monsoon a few days later. Try to put yourself back in that time, the birds, the smells, the hot air barely moving."

She inhaled deeply, eyes still closed, taking in the scent of the trees around her, listening to the sounds around them. Like one of the birds that Zack had mentioned, she mentally flew over the marsh, remembering, searching then reversing everything. She checked off the landmarks she'd already passed today until she remembered the next one, a twisted tree, slightly taller than the others nearby, its branches choked with moss, strands of it hanging so far down that they swept the ground beneath it.

She opened her eyes, scanned the trees around them, moving in a full circle once, twice and then, facing just a little bit more to the right than they'd been going before, she saw it.

"There." She pointed toward the tree, a good fifty yards away. "We need to head toward that tree."

Zack motioned to the two deputies keeping pace about twenty feet behind them now, Thomas and Carlson. They'd been assigned the task of marking their path by shoving little bright orange flag markers into the ground at regular intervals so they could easily find their way back to the road. Carlson pushed one of the flags into the ground and they all started forward again.

The two Wildlife officers—Jasper and Gene—were keeping pace on a parallel path, only occasionally visible through breaks in the trees. They were looking out for traps, footprints, wild animals—anything that might pose a threat. It was their responsibility to keep checking every few minutes on the rest of them, so they wouldn't get lost. But the two WWF officers were so stealthy and good at blending in with their surroundings that Kaylee rarely noticed when they stepped through the trees, checking on them. Then they'd be off again.

The tension that had been jumbling up Kaylee's thoughts had miraculously drained away as she'd tried to put herself back in the moment, back in time in this same place, but with Zack at her side to keep her safe. The landmarks were coming fast and clear now and she picked up her pace.

"You have a gift," she said, glancing up at Zack

before looking back at the sometimes rocky, sometimes muddy, terrain they were passing over.

"A gift?" He steadied her with his hands at her waist when she would have fallen then quickly dropped his hands to his sides.

"Your voice, the tone, the way you speak, even the words you choose…they're soothing, reassuring. You make me feel safe, and it helps me remember." She shrugged. "You have a gift."

He smiled and held up a low-hanging branch for her to pass under. "I'll have to remember that the next time one of the residents of Mystic Glades tries to whack me over the head with a beer bottle, or leads me on a merry chase through mud puddles and potholes big enough to swallow me whole, or takes all the lug nuts off the wheels on my car and stands there laughing when I back up and all the tires fall off. I'll just calmly tell them to stop and listen to the sound of my voice and see how that goes."

"Whacks you over the head with a beer bottle? Take the lug nuts off your tires? Seriously?"

"Actually, I think it was a wine bottle."

She blinked up at him. "And these are the people you put your life on the line for?"

"Yep."

"Why? If they treated me like that, I'd quit. Go somewhere else."

"Don't think I haven't thought about it. I certainly haven't had the welcome that I expected, especially since the town spent months trying to lure someone into being the chief of police, to start a brand-new police station where they've never had one before."

They reached the twisted, moss-covered tree and she didn't hesitate, waving them forward as she turned slightly to the left, heading to the next landmark. "Where were you before you took the job as chief?"

"Western Kentucky, outside of Murray. I'm a farm boy, born and raised." His smile faded. "But I was ready for a change. Honestly, I practically jumped at the chance to leave."

"Because of Jo Lynne?" she asked quietly.

He nodded and didn't say anything for a few minutes. But then he smiled again. "I like Mystic Glades, like the people, even when they're playing their practical jokes. Because beneath it all, I understand them. They're afraid of change. And they hate to admit that they need help. I figure in a few more months, once I've got some deputies hired and everyone is used to us, it will all settle down."

She eyed him in surprise. "You sound almost wistful. You actually miss them, don't you?"

He shook his head, as if surprised himself. "Yeah. I guess I do. I've made some good friends there— Jake Young, who used to be a cop himself, Dex Lassiter, who doesn't live there anymore but visits often enough to claim residence status. And of course Cole. They're good people. And they've married incredibly smart, equally good women—Faye, Amber, Silver. I think you'd really like them if you ever have a chance to meet them."

"I'd like that."

He smiled then sobered as he kept an eye on their surroundings.

They were silent again as she focused on remembering—reminding herself to use the sounds and smells to ground her memories. And then the terrain became harder and harder to travel through because the ground was wet and sucked at their feet, slowing them down. An hour passed, two, and still they kept going.

At one point Zack announced that they'd gone beyond where the original search had stopped. He asked her if she had any idea how much farther away the *camp* might be. But that wasn't a question that she could answer. There was no real sense of time or even direction in her memories, only puzzle pieces that dropped into place with each step she took.

There was a brief stop for lunch, courtesy of bottles of water and sandwiches the two deputies carried in their packs for everyone. And then they were moving again.

A few hours later, Zack touched her arm, capturing her attention.

"We'll have to turn back soon," he said. "I don't want us out here after dark. And even though the return trip will be much faster since we've marked the path, it will still take several hours to reach the road, even if we run the whole way."

She nodded, disappointment coiling in her stomach. "Can we keep going a little longer?"

He eyed the sun, glanced back at the two deputies. "All right. Another half hour, at most."

Without another word, she started off again. It wasn't long before a deep sense of foreboding passed through her and a shiver jolted straight down her spine. A mixture of dread and excitement had the hairs standing up on the back of her neck, goose bumps rising on her arms.

"We're close," she whispered. "I can feel it."

He tensed beside her, his right hand dropping down by his gun as they continued forward. They stepped through a cluster of oak trees and suddenly they were in a large clearing. Kaylee stumbled to a halt, pressing both hands against her chest, her heart pounding so hard that she felt dizzy.

"This is it. We're here."

Zack motioned to the deputies. Carlson flanked her left side. Thomas stepped up behind her. All three of them pulled their guns, keeping them pointed down at their sides, but at the ready.

She was surrounded by a wall of bodies, each with pistols, and yet she felt vulnerable, exposed, on the edge of hysteria, like she might run away screaming and tearing at her hair like a crazy woman at any moment.

"It's okay. You're safe," Zack whispered, his free hand going to her back, stroking lightly up and down as he murmured his litany of soothing words. But for once, she didn't feel reassured.

She shivered and looked around the clearing. But she didn't see it the way it was today. She saw it the way it was the last time she was here. Lifting her hand, she pointed to the left. "Over there, that's where he kept me, in the box in the ground." She pointed to the right. "And there, that's where he would set up a campfire." Her hands shook as she wrapped them around her middle and stared straight ahead, at the scarred tree she remembered so well. But she didn't say anything else. She couldn't, not yet.

"Thomas, search for the box. Carlson, see if you can find evidence of the campfires. Be alert. If the killer heard us coming, he could be hiding close by."

The men headed off to do as Zack had directed.

"She's not here," Kaylee whispered.

"We don't know that yet. She might be in the box."

"Maybe," she allowed, but she could feel it deep in her soul that if Sue Ellen had ever been at this particular camp, that she'd been moved long ago to some other place. The whole day of trudging through the woods, slogging through the mud, had been a waste. They were no closer to finding Sue Ellen than they were this morning. Her shoulders slumped with disappointment.

Thomas rushed back toward them, his jaw set. He gave Zack a quick shake of his head.

Kaylee stared at him in confusion. "You didn't find the box?"

"No, ma'am."

"But it has to be there. This is where he held me, where he held Mary. I know it." She headed off to the left, with Zack and Thomas falling in step beside her. This time, she was sure-footed, no hesitation, her feet instinctively taking her right to the spot where she remembered being placed so many times, lowered into that dark, terrifying hole in the ground. But just as Deputy Thomas had said, there was no box, not even a depression to mark where it had been.

"I don't understand." She bent down, ran her fingers across the ground. "He must have moved the box. There's no other explanation."

Zack bent down beside her just as Carlson joined them. She and Zack both looked up in question, but Carlson shook his head, just as Thomas had done. Meaning, no campfire, no burned-out depression in the ground to mark where the killer had created his nightly fires for weeks, months. Nothing at all to show that he'd ever been here, that she and Mary had ever been here, suffering horrible punishments at the hands of their captor.

No, wait. He might have been able to hide the box, cart away the scorched earth that would have revealed where the campfires had once burned. But there was no way that he could hide everything.

She stood. "This is where he held me. And I can

prove it. This way." She marched across the clearing with all three men rushing to keep up with her. She passed the first ring of trees into the woods then abruptly stopped. She didn't have to point or say anything. And she knew, by the shocked sounds of the men beside her that they believed her now, as all of them stared at the enormous scarred fallen tree lying on the ground in front of them.

And the bloodstains soaked deep into the wood.

Zack looked down at her. She could feel, sense his gaze on her more than see him, because she couldn't stop staring at the tree.

"Kaylee," he said, his voice tight, raw. "You did good. We'll get the CSU team out here. The forensic evidence will help us put him away once we find him."

"What are those marks all over the log?" Deputy Carlson asked. "Where the bark is missing in chunks?"

"That's from the chains," she said, her lower lip trembling. "He tied me up to the log with chains, put a gag over my mouth. And then, then he'd…" Her voice trailed off and suddenly she was shaking so hard that her knees knocked together. She could feel the strength giving out in her legs.

Zack swore and caught her in his arms just as she started to fall, lifting her up against his chest. "Carlson, mark this spot with a dozen of those flags. Thomas, take pictures of everything that you can, but watch your step. We need to preserve as much of the scene as possible. I'll start back with Miss Brighton. Both of you catch up as soon as you can."

Without waiting for their replies, he took off, heading back into the clearing again, his steps sure and fast as he strode back the way they'd come, holding Kaylee as though she weighed nothing. His pistol was still in his right hand even though he carried her. He wasn't taking any chances.

She clung to him, her arms tight around his neck, her cheek pressed against his chest. "Did you see the tree behind the fallen log?" she whispered. "When I made him angry, if I didn't do something he wanted fast enough, he would loop the ends of the chains over that tree's branches. Then he would—"

"Kaylee, you don't have to tell me—"

"—haul me up, several feet off the ground by my wrists and ankles, until I begged for mercy. He broke me." She couldn't help it; she started crying.

He swore and stopped, looking down at her in his arms. "No," he said, his voice gentle. "He didn't break you. You survived. And you came back to point the finger at him, to give us the evidence we'll need to capture him and put him away so he can never hurt anyone else ever again. You're the victor here, Kaylee. And we're going to find him. I promise."

She nodded miserably, wiping at the tears on her cheeks. She wasn't sure that she really believed him. But he sounded like he believed what he was saying. And for now, that had to be enough. She let out a shaky breath then pushed at his chest.

"Put me down. Please. I can stand on my own now. I can walk."

He didn't look like he believed her but he did as she said, keeping one hand at her waist, the other holding his gun pointed at the ground.

Thomas and Carlson joined them then.

"Done?" Zack asked.

"I've got a boatload of pictures," Carlson said.

Thomas held up the remaining orange flags. "And I lit up the whole area like an airport runway. We'll be able to find it again in the morning. No problem."

"Then let's get out of here."

Their little group started off again, and in spite of Zack's concerned looks toward Kaylee, she held her own just fine. She was embarrassed that she'd broken down like that. And she was determined not to slow them down again or be responsible for them being caught out here after dark. She moved as quickly as she could, and they made good time heading back toward the road.

A few minutes later Gene stepped through the trees on one of his checks. He spoke to Zack, who hung back with him behind the others, both of them exchanging information about their individual searches and the results.

Kaylee glanced back as Zack joined her again, just in time to see Gene disappear back through the trees.

"He's not coming with us?" she asked.

"He is. But he has to let Jasper know to stop worrying about the parallel path. They haven't found anything of use or concern, anyway. We might as well all stick together and make faster time."

She nodded and everyone seemed to silently agree to quicken their pace, because they were moving even faster now. All of them wanted to get as far from these woods as they could, as quickly as they could.

But after about ten minutes had passed, Zack drew them to a halt, frowning as he peered at the trees around them.

"Why haven't Gene and Jasper joined us yet?" he asked.

Thomas and Carlson looked around, the same worried expressions on their faces as on Zack's.

"Something's wrong," Zack whispered, as he raised his gun. "Listen."

Kaylee blinked at the pistol then strained to hear whatever he'd heard.

"It's too quiet," he finally said.

The two deputies raised their guns, too, glancing around, studying the trees around them.

Kaylee bit her lip and wrapped her arms around her middle. Her stomach churned as a feeling of nausea settled inside her. She didn't know if she was sensing what Zack was sensing or if his nervousness was just transmitting to her. But all of a sudden she felt borderline terrified, expecting the devil to step out from behind a tree at any moment and grab her, laughing his horrible laugh, glaring at her and promising retribution for her sins.

"Stay here," he ordered the two deputies. "I'm going to look for Gene and Jasper."

Panic bubbled up inside Kaylee. *No, don't leave me.* But he was already gone. She stared at the spot where he'd disappeared between two trees, and desperately tried not to give in to the terror that was starting to make her entire body shake. But she wasn't just scared for herself. This time she was scared for someone else…for Zack. He was risking his life out here for her. All of these men were. And if something happened to any of them she could never forgive herself.

A guttural shout sounded from the woods. Then a bloodcurdling scream.

Kaylee gasped as the two men looked at each other, eyes wide. Another scream sounded. The men each grabbed one of Kaylee's arms and took off running toward the sound of the screams.

Chapter Thirteen

Zack dropped to the ground beside Gene, who was bound at the ankles and wrists with plastic zip ties, his face bloody, a black cloth tied over his mouth. Zack yanked the gag down and ran his hands over Gene's face, his arms, searching for the source of the blood but not seeing it.

"You okay? Where are you cut?"

Gene shook his head. "I'm not hurt. It's not my blood."

Zack looked around then drew a knife from his boot and went to work on the zip ties on Gene's wrists. "Jasper? It's his blood?"

Gene nodded. "Has to be. I was walking ahead of him, just a few feet. And I felt a rush of air, whirled around. Someone hit me with a fist or a tree branch, don't know. I fell back and a guy jumped me, had the gag on before I could even draw a breath to shout out. Trussed me up like a stupid animal. A pro, I'm telling you. Only took him a matter of seconds. And then he was gone." He rubbed his wrists while Zack went to work on the ties at his ankles.

"The screams," Zack said. "Jasper?"

"Wasn't me. Like I said, didn't get a chance to say anything, let alone scream."

Zack slid the knife into his boot and helped the other man up, just as the sound of pounding feet carried to them. He yanked his gun out of the holster and whirled around, pointing at the trees just as Carlson, Thomas and Kaylee burst onto the path.

"Whoa, whoa, whoa," Carlson said, holding his hands up.

Zack let out an aggravated breath and holstered his gun. After a quick glance at Kaylee to make sure she was okay, he turned back to Gene. "Direction?"

Gene studied the trees, orienting himself, then pointed. "There. See how the grass is flattened to the right of that tree? That has to be where he went."

"Where who went?" Carlson demanded. "Jasper?"

"Jasper and the man who attacked him and Gene," Zack clarified. "Did you see his face? Can you describe him, Gene?"

The older man shook his head. "All I saw was someone dressed in black, about six-foot tall, fit, strong. His face was covered with a mask of sorts, like a ski mask, but leather or something."

Kaylee sucked in a breath, her eyes widening.

Zack waved toward the flattened patch of grass. "Thomas, you and Carlson head out, stay together, watch your backs. If you don't find Jasper or a clear trail in five minutes, head back. Strike that. Even if you find a trail, head back. Five minutes max or we come looking for you. This guy knows these woods like the back of his hand, and I'd bet anything that he was waiting for us. He planned this. He's playing us. It smells like a trap. Five minutes. Got it?"

They both nodded and took off.

Gene seemed a bit unsteady on his feet after being tied up, so Zack held on to the man's arm, waiting for him to gather himself. Kaylee stood too far away for Zack's comfort. She'd stopped as soon as she saw Gene and the blood on his face, her own face going pale.

"Kaylee, come here." He kept his tone low, gentle, trying to calm her.

She blinked, as if just realizing that she was basically alone, then hurried over to them. The dazed look on her face faded as she observed Gene. In an instant, the scared-looking vulnerable woman was replaced with a confident-looking one, ready to go into battle. Or at least, help a man who was down.

"Gene, where are you hurt?" she demanded, much as Zack had earlier.

After assuring her that he wasn't, the now red-faced Gene shoved away from Zack. Being fussed over by the woman who'd survived months of captivity, probably by the same man who'd just attacked Gene, had him looking painfully embarrassed.

Zack left the two of them speaking in low tones while he studied the ground, examining the shoe prints and broken branches and flattened grass that told the story of what had happened here. But the story didn't make sense.

He crouched down, looking at the last spot where Jasper and Gene's prints looked "normal," with one set slightly ahead of the other. That matched what Gene had said, that he was walking in front of Jasper. But what didn't fit was the lack of prints to show where the masked man had come into the picture. It was as if he'd swooped down from the trees to first grab Jasper then Gene. Where were *his* footprints?

A host of other questions raced through his mind. Why would the killer tie up Gene and take Jasper with him? Why not tie up both men, or just kill them? Had he left Gene as a warning? Had he taken Jasper as his hostage in case they caught up to him? Zack had far too many questions and not nearly enough answers.

The rustling of branches not far away had him straightening, his pistol pointed down at the ground.

"It's Thomas and Carlson," a voice rang out.

"All right," Zack called back, waiting until the two men stepped between some trees into plain sight before holstering his weapon. He didn't have to ask to know that something bad had happened. He could tell by the pallor of their skin. "What did you find?"

Carlson's jaw clenched. It was Thomas who answered, after a quick, uncomfortable look toward Kaylee.

"Blood, lots of it. Footprints. Matted-down grass, broken twigs. Drag marks."

There was something else the man wasn't telling him. "Pictures?"

In answer, Carlson held up his phone. He handed it to Zack, who quickly flipped through what Carlson had snapped. He handed the phone back to him, gave him a curt nod.

"All right," Zack said. "It's going to get dark soon and we're sitting ducks out here. We've got to get back to the road and get the word out, get some dogs and local trackers out here fast." Knowing it was probably useless, he yanked out his cell phone to check for service. But as he'd expected, there were no bars. He shoved the phone back in his holder. "Let's go."

They took off at a quick clip, using the orange marker flags as their guides. Carlson, Thomas, and Gene took turns taking up the rear, fanning out on either side of the trail, on the lookout for a possible ambush. Zack stayed by Kaylee. Within just a few hours, including several stops to catch their breath, they'd reached the road. Gene hurried to get into his truck, ready to follow them. Carlson and Thomas climbed into the back of Zack's four-wheel drive.

Zack tried his phone one more time as he stood by the passenger door, keeping a lookout while Kaylee climbed into the truck. But just as before, no bars, no signal. He put the phone away, hurried around to the driver's side and as soon as they were all in, he stomped the gas.

Dirt and gravel flew out from underneath his

tires as the truck's wheels spun then grabbed, shooting them forward. Ten long minutes later his phone chimed, letting him know he had a text message, which meant he had phone service. He yanked his phone out and made the call to Cole.

Glancing at Kaylee, who was watching him with scared, wide eyes, he realized he needed to be careful about what he said. As soon as Cole came on the line, he told him what had happened, mostly using the "ten" codes that officers used to report what they'd found. The last code he used was one that had Cole cursing into the phone—the code for dead body found.

"Who?" Cole demanded. "Jasper?"

"Negative."

A pause, then "Oh, no."

"Yep," Zack confirmed. Neither of them said the rest. They didn't have to. There was only one other person they both knew of who might be in these woods; the person in the pictures on Carlson's phone.

Sue Ellen Fullerton.

"We'll need search dogs to find Jasper," Zack said. "Can't wait for daylight. We'll need portable lights for the searchers and CSU team, skilled trackers to keep everyone from stumbling onto a gator or someone's overgrown pet python they released out here. Maybe some of those highway construction lights could be used to set up a base of operations out on the road."

"On it. I'll call Fish and Wildlife, too, have them notify the family that Jasper's missing, and also see if we can get more of their guys out here to help with the search. They'll be able to outtrack our guys. And they'll know the nighttime dangers out in the swamp way better than us, too."

"Sounds good. I'm not stopping at the temporary search base. I'm bringing Kaylee straight to the sheriff's office. I don't want her anywhere near this place." He glanced at her, giving her a hard look. "And if she fights me on that, I'll personally lock her up in a jail cell and throw away the key."

She gave him a mutinous look, but he didn't cave this time. Been there, done that and look at what had happened. She'd been within fifty yards of the killer, because that was about how far away Jasper was when he'd been taken. That probably hadn't occurred to her yet, and he hoped it never did. But no way would he take her back out there, under any circumstances. As far as he was concerned, until the killer was caught, she was going to be watched 24/7, by an armed guard of some kind.

"Zack," Cole said. "There've been a few more developments in the case since you left this morning."

Zack listened with growing anger as Cole updated him on the investigation. By the time his friend was through, Zack was livid.

"What else has happened?" Kaylee said from beside him.

There was a catch in her voice, and he realized she was frightened. He drew a deep breath then another, and forced himself to keep a carefully blank expression.

"I'll tell you in a minute." He forced a smile. "Go on," he told Cole, wanting him to finish so he could figure out for himself what his next step should be.

"I don't think it's safe bringing Miss Brighton back to the office just yet," Cole said. "Just in case someone's watching the place, assuming she'll show up there. Maybe you can take her to a hotel, a different one from last night, just to be safe. And hide out until we find this guy."

"Agreed." He checked his watch. "I'll call you once we're settled, shouldn't be more than an hour."

"Sounds good." He listened to Cole's suggestions of places to stay.

Kaylee was still watching him curiously as he pulled out onto Alligator Alley heading west toward Naples. A quick look in his rearview mirror to make sure that Gene was following them had him realizing that Carlson and Thomas were perked up and listening just as closely as Kaylee had. They knew something was up, and they were obviously waiting to see what he'd let slip if not outright share.

There was a reason he normally preferred to work alone.

He ended the call with Cole. But before anyone could ask him for an update, he made another quick call—to Gene Theroux. A few seconds later both trucks pulled to the shoulder of the highway and stopped.

"What's going on?" Deputy Thomas asked. "Car trouble?"

"No. Kaylee and I aren't going back to the sheriff's office just yet. So Gene's going to take you two back there. I don't want to delay either of you in helping with the search for Jasper."

As soon as he mentioned the missing officer, both Carlson and Thomas were more than happy to high-tail it back to Gene's truck. Soon the three men pulled out onto the highway heading toward the sheriff's office.

After waiting for a semitruck to pass, Zack pulled out, too.

"Zack, what's going on?" Kaylee asked. "I'm really getting nervous over here."

He placed his right hand on the seat between them, palm up. As he'd hoped, she put her hand in his, lacing their fingers together. Her constant trust in him was humbling.

"First, we're going to eat something and relax in an out-of-the-way restaurant. We're going to let all of the stress of today fade away and talk about something other than the case. Cole has everything in hand. He's calling in manpower from neighboring communities and amassing a search like this area has never seen. They'll find Jasper, make no mistake."

Her fingers tightened around his. "You said *first*. That implies a *second*."

"Right. Second, we go find another hotel for the night."

"Another hotel? I thought you liked the one we stayed at last night, because of the proximity to the sheriff's office."

"Yeah, well. Things have changed. Turns out I'd rather find a new place to stay."

"Zack, what's going on? Why are you afraid to take me to the sheriff's office? And don't tell me that I have to wait through dinner to find out the details. I'm not even hungry. You might as well tell me right now. What did Cole say about the investigation that you don't want me to know about?"

He sighed, feeling the weight of everything his friend had just told him, and wishing there was some way to avoid breaking the news to Kaylee. But he knew, if the roles were reversed, he'd want to know. And she *did* deserve to know. He just hated piling more on after the harrowing events of today.

He glanced over at her, at her searching gaze, then nodded and looked back at the road. A rest stop was coming up on their right, so he put his blinker on, slowed and took the exit. A few minutes later he parked his truck in the relative privacy of the back parking lot, behind the main building that housed the bathrooms, but far enough away from other cars that no one paid them any attention.

After cutting the engine, he turned in his seat to face her, and she looked up at him expectantly.

"First things first," he said. "The only person those search parties will be looking for tonight is the missing FFW officer. Sue Ellen Fullerton has already been found."

Her eyes widened. "What? That's great. Where did they find her? Is she okay? What happened…" Her smile faded and her voice trailed off as she finally took in the somberness of his voice, the lack of an answering smile on his face. "Oh, Zack. Please don't say that she's…that she—"

"I'm sorry, Kaylee. When Deputy Thomas and Carlson went looking for Jasper, they found Sue Ellen."

"But…but how did you know?"

"His phone. Carlson took pictures and showed me. There's no question that it's her."

She closed her eyes and a ragged breath escaped her. "I never saw her. When he had me in that box, the only other person I ever saw was Mary. I didn't know that he had someone else." A tear leaked out from the corner of her eye and slid down her cheek.

That tear had him aching to pull her into his arms, to hold her. Would she let him? Would she welcome his touch, take the comfort he offered? Or would it frighten her to be held by him, by any man? He hated to see her suffering and wanted to help. But he didn't know how, not with everything that had happened to her. So he forced his hands to remain in his lap and waited for her to look at him again.

When she finally wiped the tears from her cheeks and opened her over-bright eyes, she straightened her shoulders, as if bracing herself for more bad news.

"Go on," she said. "I know there's more, or you'd have taken me to the sheriff's office to tell me about Sue Ellen. Please. Just get it over with, rip off the bandage all at once. I can't take wondering anymore. I need to know what's going on."

"It's about your friend, Sandy Gonzalez. She's—"

"Is she okay? What's happened to her? Tell me."

"She's fine, more or less. Kaylee, Sandy has been arrested. She's a part of all of this."

She let out a snort of laughter then sobered. "What are you saying? That doesn't make any sense."

He rested his right arm across the seat back. "Remember this morning, that Cole had discovered that she owned the agencies used by you, Mary and Sue Ellen? It seemed like an odd coincidence. And then you talked about how the bad press had devastated your friend, that it ruined business, that it didn't make sense that she'd be involved in any way in the abductions because she had no motive, nothing to gain. Everything to lose. Well that got Cole thinking, so he had his team dig even deeper into the financials. Sure enough, just last week Sandy filed an insurance claim on behalf of her Miami company—Aventuras Travel Agency."

"Insurance? Like to help cover losses if something bad happened to one of her clients?"

"Yes and no. That kind of policy is typical, and normally pays out only if the client sues, which you haven't done. This was a special kind of policy. Instead of insuring against losses resulting from a lawsuit, this one insures against the loss of what's called 'goodwill,' basically the reputation of the company. A monetary value is placed on that reputation, the company's brand. And if the policy holder can prove the brand has been significantly damaged—as it was when the bad press was printed about your abduction—the policy pays out. And not just a little bit. The value of that policy on Aventuras is a cool one million dollars."

Kaylee's mouth fell open in shock, then she shook her head. "Wait. Hold it. That still doesn't mean she had anything to do with my abduction. What's the connection? What are you saying?"

"She had goodwill policies on all three agencies, Kaylee. She stands to collect three million dollars, all because each one of her agencies had one of their clients abducted while on a trip the agencies arranged. Now, tell me. Do you believe in coincidences to that degree? And don't forget that she hid the fact that she owned all three companies. It makes sense that she would have created those shell companies for this very purpose, to hide her connection so no one would put two and two together. She even purchased the policies from three different insurance companies. She did everything she could to hide the connections, hoping no one would ever think to look."

Kaylee shook her head vigorously, but she'd gone pale. She might be in denial, but the truth was sinking in whether she wanted it to or not. "Wait. Okay, I agree it sounds crazy. But how does it play out? She looks up serial killers on the internet somewhere and hires one of them to take out three of her clients? Come on, Zack. That's ridiculous. There has to be another explanation."

"Oh, there is. His name is Hutch Mulcahy. He's Sandy's ex-husband, who's also an ex-con. He's been in prison for ten years and got out about six months ago, which is right around the time that Sandy created those shell companies and purchased her 'goodwill' insurance. Sandy and Hutch made plans to destroy the reputation of her three companies so they could collect on the insurance. And as soon as they collected, they were going to skip the country and live happily ever after."

Kaylee pressed her hands against her temples and shook her head. "No, no, that can't be. I've known Sandy for years. And I never heard about an ex-husband."

He shrugged. "I'm sure she wasn't going to brag about having been married to a man who went to prison for rape."

She slowly lowered her hands. "Rape?"

"Among other things, yes." At her crestfallen look, he said, "Kaylee, I'm so sorry that you have to hear it like this. I wanted to break it to you at the hotel, talk it through. But you wanted to know right now what was going on. I just wish there was something I could have done to soften the blow. Sandy Gonzalez is behind your abduction and the abductions and murders of Mary and Sue Ellen. She colluded with her ex-husband to have something bad happen to each of you so they could collect their millions and run off."

Tears were falling faster and unchecked now. Her lower lip trembled. "But she's a woman, and a friend. I can't believe she would wish what happened to me, to those other women, on any of us. I just can't see it."

"Some of the details are still fuzzy," he allowed. "She's admitted to the collusion to cash in on her goodwill policy, and that her ex-con ex-husband was supposed to help with that. But you're right, she swears she would never agree to what happened to any of you. She's placing all of the blame squarely on her ex, saying he was supposed to do something much more mild, like hold you up at gunpoint, slash your rental car's tires, that sort of thing. She claims she had no idea he was this evil, that he'd go this far."

She was holding it together by a thread. He could see that in how alarmingly pale she looked, how wild her eyes were and how violently she trembled. But she still wasn't giving in to her turmoil. Perhaps it was the past month spent wondering why she'd been targeted that had her pushing through the pain, continuing to insist on answers now.

"Hutch Mulcahy?" she whispered. "That's his name? The man who…the man who…hurt me? Who killed those women? And kidnapped Jasper?"

"We believe so, yes. He matches the description you gave—height, weight, Caucasian. Cole's looking into whether there's a recording of his voice on file with the Department of Corrections so you can listen to it, see if it sounds familiar. And there's a BOLO out on him."

"BOLO?"

"Cop speak. Means be on the lookout. Kind of like an Amber Alert except it's only sent to law enforcement, not the public. Every officer in the state will be shown his picture so they can keep an eye out for him. And Cole's men will figure out every step the man's taken since he got out of prison. Don't worry. They'll get him."

She nodded but didn't look convinced. He supposed it made sense that she'd still be frightened, worried. Until Mulcahy was behind bars, she'd see him in every shadow, hear him in every footstep behind her, never be able to relax or feel safe.

"It'll all work out," he tried to reassure her. "Cole's men will find Jasper, and they'll find Mulcahy. And you'll never have to worry about him again." When she didn't say anything, just stared out the windshield as if lost in thought, he started up the engine. "Come on. We'll go get a suite at some fancy hotel downtown and get cleaned up. I'll even let you pay for the room if that will make you happy."

That finally made her smile, even if it was only a half-smile. "In that case, let's go to the Ritz-Carlton. I want to soak in a deep tub full of bubbles and high-powered jets to soothe my aching muscles. I'm not used to all the walking, not to mention jogging, that we did today."

Her smile faded and he knew she was thinking about Sue Ellen and the missing FFW officer. Since there was nothing else he could say that would ease those hurts, he backed out of the parking space to head back to the highway.

A horn blared. Tires screeched. Zack jerked his head around just in time to see a white panel van barrel into the side of his pickup, just missing his door. Kaylee screamed as glass shattered from both vehicles and tinkled all over the pavement. The front hood had crumpled up at a crazy angle and bright green radiator fluid shot up like a geyser.

He checked Kaylee. "You okay?"

She was shaking, pale, but nodded. "I'm... I'm okay. You?"

"Fine." He frowned, staring through the hole where the windshield used to be. "But my truck's not."

A muffled moan carried to them from the other vehicle. Because of the angle, he couldn't see the person or people in the van. But that moan didn't sound good.

"Stay here. I'll check on the other driver."

He tried to open his door but it resisted his efforts. He gritted his teeth in disgust and shoved the door, hard. It finally opened with a sickening metallic screech. After hopping down, he rounded the back of the van.

A loud crack, something zipping through the air, and then burning, agonizing pain. Zack fell to the asphalt, convulsing, white-hot agony ripping through every nerve, his teeth grinding so hard they seemed in danger of breaking. And then suddenly, the pain stopped, leaving him sweating and panting on the ground. He blinked as his still pain-fogged mind registered what had happened—he'd been Tased. This wasn't an accident. It was a trap. Kaylee! He had to protect Kaylee.

He shoved himself up off the ground, staggered, caught himself against the back of the van. Twin darts with thin wires attached protruded from his thigh. He grabbed for one of them just as the loud crack of electricity sizzled in the air again. Immediately, he fell to the ground again, his fingers curling like talons as the blazing pain shredded his nerves, making him helpless, worthless, as someone leaned past him and opened the van doors. His attacker tossed something in the back that landed with a loud thump. Kaylee. And she hadn't been moving.

Fighting against the blistering pain, Zack desperately tried to grab his gun, but his whole body was convulsing and he couldn't manage it. The man who'd taken Kaylee leaned over him. Zack vaguely registered the dark mask over the man's face before he plunged a needle into Zack's neck. The electricity running through his body abruptly stopped and he lay there once again, breathing hard, his body wrung out and exhausted as if he'd been running a marathon. He grabbed the darts, yanking them out and tossing them away. He shoved himself up into a crouch, ready to launch himself at the man who'd jumped back several feet.

A wave of dizziness had him falling to the ground. He shook his head, desperately trying to focus and fight off whatever the masked man had drugged him with. But in spite of his feverish efforts, the relentless darkness won. As he surrendered to unconsciousness, a last thought flitted through his mind.

The devil had them.

Chapter Fourteen

A groan sounded nearby. Zack frowned, then his face heated as he realized that he was the one who'd made that pathetic sound. Every inch of his body hurt, as if it were one big bruise. His mind was a confusing fog of impressions. Everything seemed disconnected, fuzzy, and he couldn't focus his thoughts. His mouth was dry, his stomach roiling with nausea. Drugged. The way he felt, he'd definitely been drugged.

A mask, with holes for eyes, a wide slit for the mouth. A man, carrying Kaylee, dumping her inside...what? The trunk of a car? No. That wasn't right. Crunching metal, shattering glass, a zapping, buzzing sound. Pain. Unbearable, scorching pain. His left thigh ached, burned. He rubbed his arm across his jeans, felt the holes in the cloth.

Everything snapped together in his mind. The van, slamming into his truck. Him, rounding the back. Wires shooting toward him, electricity sizzling through his nerves. A man, dressed all in black, leather mask concealing his features. And Kaylee, unconscious…or worse…tossed like a rag doll into the back of the van.

His eyes flew open, but he saw nothing but darkness—complete, absolute darkness. Could it be nighttime already? Or was he in the trunk of a car, or lying on the floor of the cargo van? Kaylee. Where was she? He had to find her, help her.

He tried to sit up but his head banged against something directly above him. He cursed and fell back, throwing his hands out, surprised to find something hard and flat blocking him. He jerked his legs, same thing, blocked by walls all around. Beneath him, beside him, above him. Like a…coffin. Confusion was swept away and he realized with agonizing certainty exactly what had happened. He was inside one of those boxes that Kaylee had described, probably just below the ground.

The devil had him.

The hell with that. He had to get out of here, find Kaylee. He shoved against the smooth lid of the box, his muscles straining. A creak. Did something give? If this was one of the same Plexiglas boxes the killer had been using all along, maybe the seals were beginning to weaken from age and the elements. If Zack could just get the right leverage, maybe he could use the metal stem of his belt buckle to jam into the seam, score it, so he could break the lid off the box.

He drew a deep breath, grimacing at the hot, musty quality of the air, and then strained against the lid again. He tried lifting his knees against it, too, but the box was too small; he couldn't lift his legs enough to get leverage. Instead, he continued to push his forearms against the lid, his arms shaking from the prolonged effort. Another creak.

The darkness suddenly gave way to light. Zack squinted against the sun as it poured down through overhead branches. But he didn't see anyone above him, just the Plexiglas top of the box and trees. He was buried in the ground, just below the surface. Spindly moss-covered oaks formed the canopy above, along with the twisted branches of cypress trees. The cypress, that musty smell…he was in the Everglades. Which meant Kaylee must be here, too, thrust back into her worst nightmare. Was she in another box? Was their captor nearby? He must be, to have removed whatever had covered the top of Zack's box.

A footstep, another, then the sun was blocked out again, this time by the silhouette of a man bending over him. Zack blinked as his eyes refocused without the sun in them. The man was wearing a leather mask, the same one from back at the van. It covered his head so that Zack couldn't see the man's hair or any part of his face except his mouth, and a small patch of skin visible just above where the mask tied at his throat. Caucasian—he was white, like Kaylee's attacker. And large, about Zack's size. He wore a black T-shirt, black pants, gloves.

"Trying to memorize me in case you ever get me into a lineup?" the man's voice rasped above him.

"Where's Kaylee?" Zack demanded, still searching for details, anything that he could use to identify the man. Was that a mole on his throat, barely visible above the leather tie that secured the mask? Yes. But there was nothing else distinctive in that small patch of skin.

"Worried about your girlfriend?" Laughter wheezed above him. "Don't worry. I'm going to give her some very special attention." He stroked the top of the box like a lover, his hands smoothing over the thick plastic, his fingers poking at the holes that allowed air inside. Then his smile faded and he leaned down within a few inches of the box, his dark eyes flashing with anger. "You and your nonstop persistence have ruined my fun. I'm going to have to find a new playground." His lips curved again. "But not before one last hurrah."

He rolled away from the opening, leaving the sunlight blinding Zack again. Zack raised a hand to shade his eyes then pounded against the top of the box. "Come back here," he yelled. "Face me like a man instead of slinking away like a coward."

Footsteps sounded, going away this time, followed by laughter.

"Come back. Do you hear me, you animal?" Zack slammed his forearm against the lid.

Sounds, from close by. Someone scrabbling in the dirt?

"Well, hello there, dear," the masked man's voice taunted, but Zack couldn't see him. "It's been far too long, my little escape artist." His voice turned menacing at that last part, and angry.

Another scrabbling sound, a click and then a terrified scream.

Kaylee.

KAYLEE BIT HER lip to keep from crying out again. Her shoulder throbbed from the devil grabbing her by one arm and yanking her up out of the box. That was when she'd screamed, and now her left arm hung at an awkward angle at her side, useless—dislocated probably. Every time her arm moved, pain radiated outward like a knife cutting into her. She tried to hold it tight against her body but there was no way to keep it completely immobile, not with the devil tugging her other arm, forcing her to stumble through the woods after him.

She glanced back once, looking for Zack, hoping, praying he was still alive. But she didn't see him anywhere, hadn't seen him since the devil had staged that car accident and ripped her door open, plunging a needle deep into her neck.

"Hurry up," he ordered, his voice raspy as he yanked her good arm.

Pain lanced through her shoulder. She bit down

harder and the metallic taste of blood filled her mouth. In all of her nightmares at home, she'd always remembered what had already happened, thinking nothing could be that bad again. But she'd never, not once, considered that she'd ever be back in this man's clutches. She'd never seen a future where this could happen.

A whimper escaped between her clenched teeth before she could stop it.

The devil glanced back, his mouth tilting into a cruel smile. And beyond him, she could see a scarred, twisted tree much like the ones from before, at the other *camps* where he'd held her, and chained her and…hurt her.

He was going to do it again, hurt her, beat her… cut her.

No!

She couldn't do this, not again. She'd rather die than let him hurt her, humiliate her, brutalize her and reduce her to the level of an abused animal, whimpering, crying, curling into herself and giving him the satisfaction of breaking her. No one had the right to hurt her like that. One way or another, this was going to end now. No matter what.

She picked her feet up and fell to the ground. The unexpected movement sent a sharp, agonizing pain shooting through her shoulder. But it also knocked her captor off balance, tearing her hand free from his grasp and making him stumble and fall against a tree.

Grabbing her bad arm with her good, Kaylee launched herself to her feet and took off running.

WHACK, WHACK, WHACK! Zack pounded the pin of his belt buckle against the seam where the two corners of the Plexiglas box met near his head. He'd been urged on by the scream that he'd heard a few minutes ago and the answering maniacal laughter coming from the man who'd abducted Kaylee and him. And then, just a few minutes after that, a guttural shout of rage followed by the sound of someone running, *two* people running, their feet pounding against the ground, heading away from him. That could only mean one thing. Kaylee had gotten away, and her abductor was chasing her.

Which meant Zack needed to get out of this box, *now*, before Kaylee's pursuer caught her. There was no way she could outrun him, not if she was barefoot, like Zack, an old trick their abductor had obviously used again to ensure that it would be difficult for them to run if they did manage to escape. Plus, that man was just as tall as Zack. His stride was much longer than Kaylee's. In a flat-out race, she didn't stand a chance.

Hide, Kaylee. Find a place to burrow down until he runs past you. Don't try to outrun him. Outthink him.

Crack. The glue holding the corner split about six inches down. He could see daylight and dirt from between the two pieces. But it wasn't enough. Not nearly enough. He pushed and strained every muscle of his body against the sides of the box and continued to pound the belt buckle against the corner seam.

QUIET. DON'T MAKE a sound, Kaylee. Breathe in, out, in, out, through your mouth. Quiet. Don't make a sound.

Kaylee's whole body shook as she huddled inside the hollowed-out, rotten tree trunk. She'd done it. Somehow, she'd managed to evade her captor. He'd run right past her after she'd ducked into this spot, tucking herself in, her knees against her chest, her hurt arm contorted and sending sharp bursts of pain through her entire body. The only pain she could remember worse than this was when the devil had cut her. So she'd just have to somehow endure, without screaming or giving voice to her agony that would give away her hiding place. Her bottom lip was practically shredded from clamping her teeth down so much to keep from crying out.

Click.

She blinked, staring out into the heavily shadowed woods around her. What was that? She held so still that her lungs started to burn, reminding her she had to take a breath. She drew air in as quietly as possible, listening intently, searching for signs of movement.

Thump, thump.

Oh, God. Was that…was that a footstep? There,

twenty feet away, a shadow moved. She looked left, the bushes were too thick. Right, she'd have to go to the right. She gritted her teeth and hauled herself up from her hiding place, all the while keeping an eye on those shadows. A dark form scurried out. She let out a squeak of alarm and then realized it was just a raccoon. Footsteps sounded not far away, pounding on the ground. No, no, no. He must have heard her. He was coming back.

She threw herself to the right and took off again.

Laughter floated to her on the warm breeze.

"I...seeeeeee...yoooooou," he taunted in a sing-song voice.

"Leave me alone, you sick pervert," she yelled back, without turning. *Faster, faster. Run!*

His roar of rage told her he didn't appreciate her insult. A smile curved her lips for the briefest moment. But just as quickly, as his footsteps pounded closer, she cursed herself for being so stupid. Taking potshots at him and making him angry only gave her satisfaction that lasted a few seconds. What he might do to her in retaliation, on the other hand, would last far longer and would, without a doubt, be excruciatingly painful.

If she even survived.

The pseudo-path she was following abruptly ended at a thick ring of trees too close together for her to pass. She whirled around, a whimper escaping as her shoulder protested the quick movement.

The devil was there, no more than ten feet in front of her. He stopped and straightened from his crouch, his cruel lips curving in delight beneath the mask, above where it tied at his throat.

"What do you want from me?" she demanded, as she inched toward her left, and the break in the trees she could sense more than see.

In answer, he slowly pulled a knife from the top of his boot, its serrated edges winking in what little fading sunlight filtered in through the branches above. He held it up, his mouth turning down at the corners into a sneer.

"Let's see just what a *pervert* can do with a knife, shall we, little Kaylee?" he rasped, his voice sending shivers of dread down her spine. "I went easy on you before, because I thought we had more time together. But your time has run out."

A scream caught in her throat, but she forced it back. *Don't give him the pleasure of hearing you scream, Kaylee. Think. Lie. Convince him, somehow, to let you go.*

"I… I know who you are," she yelled, as she edged farther left. "Sandy gave you up, told the police everything."

He stopped his forward advance, as if startled. Then he clucked his tongue, shook his head and started forward again, moving the knife back and forth, back and forth. Eight feet now, seven.

Kaylee stepped through the break in the trees, putting an extra couple of feet between them. But thick bushes scraped her back through her shirt, cutting into her skin, stopping her from going any farther. She looked around, desperate for something to use as a weapon.

"Your name is Mulcahy... Hutch Mulcahy," she said. "The police have a BOLO out on you. And they're looking for your camps, searching the swamp. They will find you, unless you go, now. Escape while you still can."

He laughed. "Trying to get rid of me, sweet Kaylee?"

"You kidnapped a cop," she continued, her gaze still darting around. "Every cop within a hundred miles of this place is searching for Jasper, and you."

He cocked his head, clucking his tongue. "It's too late to save Jasper. Far, far too late." He laughed, as if at some inside joke, and started forward again. "Come on, now. Come face your punishment." He kept inching forward, slowly bridging the distance between them. She was trapped and he knew it, and he was enjoying her fear, stringing it out, reveling in it.

Five feet. Four. He lifted the knife above his head, and she saw her death in his dark, soulless eyes.

"Don't worry," he taunted. "I'm not going to kill you. Yet. I'm going to punish you first. Slowly. And then...then, I'll kill you."

The knife came down in a slashing motion toward her good shoulder. She dodged left at the last second then dove to the ground as he whirled around, arcing the knife toward her again. She landed, hard, letting out a scream when her bad arm flung out, tearing at her shoulder. He laughed and jumped on top of her, pinning her to the ground.

And once again, he had her. Just like before, his greater weight anchoring her down, making it impossible for her to move. She stared up into his cold, dark eyes, hoping to see something, anything, of the human being that existed behind the mask. But she saw no empathy, no flicker of guilt or regret, only cold determination, and sickening triumph as he once again raised his knife above his head.

She closed her eyes. His body jerked against hers and she waited, expecting the slashing burn of the knife any second. A guttural roar of rage sounded above her and he rolled off her.

Her eyes flew open and she stared in stunned amazement to see Zack holding the devil's wrist, both men rolling on the ground, grappling for control of the knife.

"Run, Kaylee!" Zack yelled without looking at her. "Get out of here."

She braced her good hand on the tree beside her, shoving herself to her knees. She looked over her shoulder at Zack, on his back now, with the devil above him, trying to stab the knife down into Zack's throat. They were locked in a life-and-death struggle, both men seemingly equally matched, except that her captor had managed to pin Zack and was using his position on top to his advantage.

There must be something she could do. She took a wobbly step toward them.

"Run," Zack ordered again, and his gaze flitted her way, a frown wrinkling his forehead. "For God's sakes, Kaylee, get out of here."

She took off running, past the struggling men, back the other way. When she found a break in the thick trees, she headed between them.

A shout sounded behind her in the distance, followed by cursing. Then another shout, this one sounding like someone in terrible pain. Zack? Had he been hurt? Stabbed? Worse? She stumbled to a halt, clutching her bad arm against her middle. She turned around, took one step then stopped. Zack needed help. She had to help him.

Can't do it. Can't go back. Can't.

But how could she not? Somehow Zack had managed to untie himself, or perhaps get out of one of those horrible boxes, if that was where he'd been. But instead of running, escaping, saving himself, he'd run *toward* the devil…to save *her*. She couldn't leave him alone to fight, to possibly die, because of her. Hadn't she done that once before? Convincing herself she'd come back with help? Instead, by the time she'd managed to send help, it was too late. Mary had paid the price for Kaylee's poor decision, her cowardice. She couldn't let that happen again. She couldn't leave Zack.

But she was practically useless with her arm slowing her down as it was, with the pain blinding her, making mush of her thoughts. She had to do something about it. She reached up with her good hand and yanked, hard, at the row of buttons on her shirt. They popped off, flying through the air to land in the slightly damp soil. Clenching her teeth against the pain, she pulled her shirt off her good side then raked it down her bad arm in one, swift movement. A groan of agony wheezed from her, but the worst was over. Clad now only in her bra and jeans, she strung the shirt around her neck, using one hand and her teeth to put a knot in the end. Then she slid her injured hand through the loop her shirt made.

Immediately, the pressure eased and the pain cut dramatically as her arm relaxed in the makeshift sling. Now, without the pain fogging her mind, she just might be more help than hindrance. She searched the path as she started forward again. There, a short, almost straight length of branch that had broken off a tree. It was about the thickness and length of a baseball bat. With her hand around the end, letting the stick hang down by her side, she took off running toward where she'd last seen Zack, and prayed she wasn't too late.

Chapter Fifteen

Kaylee stumbled to a halt, hoisting her bat up to her shoulder when she saw the devil and Zack. They were both on their feet now, circling each other like two wrestlers, looking for an opening. Physically, they looked about evenly matched—except for the wicked-looking, eight-inch blade in the devil's hand. There was a smear of blood on Zack's right forearm, but it didn't seem to be bleeding. Kaylee looked for the source of the blood then saw it—a three-inch slash in the denim covering Zack's right thigh. Blood was oozing out, darkening his jeans.

She gasped in dismay and took a step forward.

Zack's gaze darted to her and he shouted something. Too late, she realized her mistake. The devil whirled around toward her, slashing his knife down. She swung instinctively with her makeshift bat. The knife's blade bit into the wood and glanced off.

Zack dove toward the devil just as he snatched the knife from the wood. The man yanked it up and out, catching Zack in the shoulder. Zack cursed and grabbed the man's wrist, twisting it viciously. Kaylee stumbled back, out of the way, searching for her tree branch. A pained shout sounded behind her. She turned around to see the knife go flying off into the woods. Both men grappled against each other, rolling on the path.

Kaylee found the tree branch and ran forward. As soon as the devil rolled on top of Zack, she hauled back and swung as hard as she could. He screamed in pain as it slammed into the side of his rib cage. He kicked out with both feet, shoving Zack away from him. And then he was on his feet, sprinting down the path.

Zack was slower to get up, staggering after the devil, favoring his hurt leg. Kaylee ran up to him.

"Wait, you're losing too much blood. We have to stop the bleeding."

He looked down at her, his eyes unfocused as he swayed on his feet. And then he sank to the ground, landing hard on his knees. He shook his head, obviously trying to clear his vision.

Kaylee braced him to keep him from falling. She looked toward where the devil had disappeared. She didn't hear anything. Maybe he wouldn't come back. No, she knew better. He wasn't the type to stop, to give up. He would come back. And they needed to get out of here before he did.

She set her stick on the ground beside them and checked his shoulder. "Not very deep. It's barely bleeding." She moved to his side, gently peeled the cut fabric back from the wound and winced. "But this one is bad." She pressed her hand down on the wound, trying to staunch the bleeding.

He sucked in a breath, his face going pale. His Adam's apple bobbed in his throat and then he turned his head, looking at her, his eyes just inches from hers.

"Why did you come back?" he asked, his voice tight. "I told you to run."

She gave him a sad smile. "You came for me, put your own life in danger to save me. How could I leave you?" And then, figuring life was way too short not to finally do what she'd wanted to do since waking up to see him standing guard beside her hospital bed, she closed the last few inches between them and kissed him.

He froze—in shock or disgust she wasn't sure. Embarrassed either way, she started to pull back. Then one of his hands hooked around her, pressing between her shoulder blades, and his lips moved against hers in a fiery, mind-numbing kiss. Shock then, definitely not disgust, as he deepened the kiss in a wild frenzy that had her sinking against him, wanting to get as close as possible—until her hurt arm cried out in protest.

She tore her mouth free, ignoring the sting of pain from where she'd sunk her teeth into it before, but unable to ignore the pain of her shoulder. She fell back off his lap. He frowned and caught her arm, bracing her.

"I'm sorry," she whispered. "I shouldn't have done that."

"No, you shouldn't have." His smile softened his words and he ran his thumb gently over her bruised, cut lips, making her breath catch at the soft caress. "But only because we need to get moving before he comes back. Otherwise, feel free to kiss me anytime you want." In spite of the pain he must have been in, he winked.

She felt that wink all the way to her toes. Between the kiss and that sexy look, her world had just tilted on its axis. And suddenly, she had a whole lot more to live for.

He gently shoved her back and staggered to his feet. Then he pulled her up with him. He searched the gloom around them, every muscle tense, before looking down at her again. "Your shoulder?"

"Dislocated, I think. When he yanked me up out of the box, it twisted and I felt a pop."

He frowned and ran his hand very carefully across the top of her shoulder, his touch infinitely gentle as he pressed his fingers down, feeling the damage. But still, it had her sweating just to stand there and not jerk away.

"Sorry," he said. "I can help with this, pop it back in. But it's going to hurt."

"Will I be able to use it once you do?"

"Better than you're using it now. And it won't hurt nearly as much once it's back in place."

She looked down the path. "He'll come back, won't he?"

"Count on it. We need to get out of here, get you hidden somewhere safe so I can find him and end this once and for all."

"Your leg—"

"Is fine. You stopped the bleeding."

She glanced down, surprised to see that he was right. "We still need to bind it."

"I'll tie my shirt around it. Just as soon as we take care of your arm." He leaned over her and untied the knot in her shirt, dropping it to the ground.

She grabbed her hurt arm, which was throbbing now that she didn't have the sling to keep the pressure off her shoulder.

He took her left hand in his and braced his other on her hurt shoulder.

"What are you going to—" She sucked in a breath and squeezed her eyes shut as he slowly pulled on her arm, stretching it out toward him. "It hurts, it hurts, it—" She let out a gasp as something popped.

"It's over now," he whispered, pulling her to him, cradling her against his chest. "Don't cry, Kaylee. I'm sorry that I hurt you. But it's over now."

She blinked, surprised to realize that he was right. Tears were flowing down her cheeks. But she also realized something else; she could move her hand, her arm, without pain exploding through her body. She gently shoved back from him and tested her left arm, amazed that she could lift it again. It still hurt, but more like a strained muscle than the agony she'd been in earlier. She could handle a strain.

"You fixed it." She started to lift her arm higher, testing her range of movement.

He stopped her, forcing her arm back down. "Don't. The tendons are stretched, maybe even torn. Your arm could pop out again or do even more damage if you lift it very high."

She nodded, rubbing her shoulder with her other hand. "How did you know how to do that?"

"Training, and growing up on a remote farm with three roughhousing brothers, hours away from the nearest hospital. You learn what you have to."

He picked up her crumpled shirt and shook it out before helping her into it. He smiled at the lack of buttons then grabbed the ends and tied them together.

"Best I can do," he said.

"Thank you."

He had already turned away and was searching some nearby bushes for something. A moment later he straightened, holding the knife that the devil had carried. It was stained with blood. He wiped it across his jeans then yanked his pocket inside out, letting it hang beside his leg. He cut a slit in the stitching on the top, creating a makeshift scabbard for the knife, which he slid inside.

"What are you," she asked, "former military or something?"

"Hunter," he said. "I know all the tricks. If I had the right tools—binoculars, a crossbow or a gun, I'd have taken that creep out long ago. But at least now I have the knife. Come on. We need to get moving." He held his hand out for hers.

She reached down and grabbed her stick first, held it in her still-sore left hand so she could put her right hand in his. "Where are we going?"

"I'd like to find that sick animal and take him out. But I'm not naive enough to think that all he brought with him was a knife. He planned this. He's got something else up his sleeve. And we need to get as far from here as we can, as fast as we can, before he finds us again."

His ominous words had her staring at the shadows around them in trepidation. For some reason she'd hoped that after the fight with Zack, that their captor would have realized there was too much at stake, that he'd be safer if he went back to wherever he came from. But what Zack said rang true. He'd gone to great risk ramming that van into their truck at the rest stop. Someone could have seen them, called it in. Whatever he'd brought them here to do was something he deeply wanted to do. And just because he'd lost the first round didn't mean he'd stop now. If anything, he had more incentive, more anger to feed his sickness, to make him want revenge.

"We'll head out a bit," Zack said, "then I'll find a tall tree to climb so I can see where we are, and hopefully find a road or a way out of here. Do you recognize anything around here? Is this one of the camps where he held you?"

They headed down the path, away from where the devil had run just a few minutes earlier.

She shook her head. "No. The only thing familiar is that he had me in a box and took me to one of his torture trees."

He gave her a sharp look. "Torture trees? You mean, like the one you showed me at the camp earlier today?"

She nodded. "Where he would chain me…hurt me. But he didn't get to tie me up this time. I dropped my legs out from beneath me, threw him off balance. Then I ran."

He nodded approvingly. "How did he get you, back at the rest stop? Did he taser you, too?"

"No, he stuck a needle in my neck, knocked me out. I didn't know he'd tasered you. I'm so sorry."

"It's better than a bullet. But trust me. If I get a chance to return the favor and send him on a five-second ride, let him know how it feels, I won't hesitate."

She laughed then tugged his arm to stop him. "Wait, it's too thick to get through that way," she warned. "That's where I got trapped earlier."

He nodded, studying the bushes and trees that

seemed to be closing in on them. "This way." He urged her off the path to their left, finding a gap she hadn't seen.

A deafening boom echoed through the woods, and the bark beside Zack's head seemed to explode.

He grabbed Kaylee and yanked her behind the tree just as another boom sounded. Kaylee's dazed mind finally registered what the sound was. Somebody had just shot at them.

"Run, Kaylee, run," Zack urged, pulling her with him through the thick underbrush.

This time she didn't think twice. She took off, running faster than she'd ever run in her life.

ONE THING ZACK had learned upon moving to Mystic Glades just a few months ago—there were over two and a half million acres in this endless swamp. And right now it seemed like he and Kaylee had been plopped right down into the middle of it, with no way out and a lunatic with a rifle tracking them. He hadn't told Kaylee his suspicions, and it had taken a couple of hours of running, hiding, starting, stopping, as they made their way deeper and deeper into the Everglades for him to realize exactly what was going on.

The devil was playing with them. They were being herded like sheep, and hunted.

He didn't know if that was what their pursuer had planned originally. But it was what he was doing now. He was taking potshots at trees near them every once in a while, but never hitting them. Zack didn't think either of them was lucky enough to have avoided getting hit after eight separate rifle shots. So the only alternative that made sense was that they were being hunted like wild game, being driven onward, toward some unknown goal. He had to figure out where they were, get the lay of the land and make a plan. Or neither of them was going to survive much longer.

He glanced at her walking beside him as they caught their breath from the last few minutes of running. Her eyes were haunted. Dark bruises were forming beneath them, and she looked shell-shocked, walking wounded, close to breaking down. That was what that evil maniac behind them had done, terrified her until she was on the brink of giving up, or closing in on herself, perhaps curling into a fetal position and surrendering to whatever was going to happen to them.

Well, forget that. Zack had to figure out a way to go on the offensive, to take control of this situation. He'd hoped to outrun their pursuer, find a place to put Kaylee so she'd be safe while he went after the hunter. But they couldn't seem to get far enough ahead of him to do that. Even now, the distant sound of footsteps could occasionally be heard, steadily gaining on them. And any minute, when they stepped too far left or right, too far away from the cover of trees, the rifle would boom. Bark would explode. And they'd be forced to run again. They were already so tired that just walking was a struggle. Both of them were running out of steam.

It was time to make a stand.

He looked down at his inside-out pocket, considering the knife. Taking a knife to a gunfight was a recipe for disaster, and pretty much worthless in the scheme of things. Beside him, Kaylee still clutched her stick. She'd managed to get one good wallop on their attacker earlier. But in a close fight, she'd never have enough leverage to do true damage. She was too small, and with only one good arm. Her damaged shoulder would never stand up to the strain of her using both hands to swing that stick like a bat. He'd have to leave her the knife. There was no other way.

He pulled her behind a thick tree stand, with three giant oaks giving them cover for now, until their captor caught up to them again.

"Kaylee, here."

She blinked up at him in surprise as she automatically took the knife he held out to her. But then she was shaking her head, holding the knife back out to him. "No, whatever you're wanting to try, just stop it. Take the knife back. We're in this together."

"Keep it. Make a slit in the waistband of your pants so the blade hangs out and doesn't cut your thigh. Then cover it with your shirt. He'll never expect that from you. If I fail, and he finds you, let him get in close. Act terrified—"

"Act? I don't have to act. I *am* terrified." Her eyes

were wide, her face pale, emphasizing the truth of her words.

He gently stroked her hair, wishing he had the time to tell her how much he admired her, how courageous he thought she was, how she'd made him feel things he'd never expected to feel again after losing a piece of himself when Jo Lynne had died. But there wasn't time for that, and little point. He knew the odds were against him in the fight to come. His injured leg was shaky, weak and it was taking all his strength to keep moving and not let Kaylee see that the cut was far worse than he'd been letting on. It might not be bleeding like it had been, but the damage was done, muscles cut. Add to that his cut shoulder, and side, and he was a mess. Together, continuing as they were, neither of them was going to make it. But if he went on the offensive, even if it meant sacrificing himself for her, then maybe, just maybe, she'd be able to escape. And that would make the sacrifice worth it.

"Then use that fear to your advantage," he told her. "Let him see it, gloat over it. He'll let his guard down, thinking he has you right where he wants you, too afraid to fight him. When he's close, too close to use that rifle pressing against you, that's when you feel behind you for the knife then drive it up into his belly. Shove it as hard as you can, with both hands, then rip the point of the knife up, toward his heart, from the inside. You'll cut through a slew of vital organs. There's no recovering from a gut wound like that."

She shuddered with revulsion. "I could never do that."

He firmly closed her hand around the hilt of the knife. "You can, and you will if you have to, to save your life."

"What are you planning?" she demanded.

"You're going to run, sticking close to the trees for cover, just like we've been doing. And I'm going to wait and hopefully ambush this creep."

"He's got a rifle. And you said yourself he may have other weapons, other tricks up his sleeve."

He let out a deep breath. "Kaylee, we're not going to make it the way we're going. We're tired, practically dragging. And he's still pursuing us. I have to change the status quo to give us a chance."

She glared up at him. "To give me a chance, don't you mean? You're sacrificing yourself for me. Admit it."

"I didn't say that." He glanced around the edge of the tree, worried that he hadn't heard footsteps in a while. "We don't have time for this. You need to get moving."

"No."

He frowned. "No?"

She shook her head and slid the knife into his makeshift scabbard before grabbing her stick again. "If you leave me, I'll follow you. We're in this together. No one is dying to save the other."

A footstep sounded behind them, close, but not

as close as he'd feared. "Kaylee, you're wasting time arguing with me."

"No, you're wasting time trying to figure out a way to get me to leave you. You might as well not bother." Her face twisted in misery as the brave mask she'd been wearing seemed to crack. "Zack, Mary died after I left her. I couldn't bear it if you died because you were trying to give me a better chance at escape. Please, don't do this. Let's stick together. There has to be another way to defeat him."

He stared down at her then finally shook his head. "You're incredibly stubborn, you know that?"

"So I've been told."

He listened to the sounds of pursuit getting closer, all the while racking his brain, trying to come up with a better plan, something Kaylee might not fight him about. Finally, he looked down at her. "It's dangerous, and not much better than my original plan."

"We're already in danger," she said. "Does this new plan involve us sticking together?"

"Yes and no."

Her brows drew down.

He leaned around the tree again then jerked back. "All right. This is what we're going to do."

Chapter Sixteen

As plans went, it wasn't much, Kaylee supposed. And it was scary, too, since it involved her staying on the ground while Zack perched in the tree above, ready to drop down onto their pursuer. But since she hadn't been able to think of anything better, and she refused to let Zack run off without her to face the devil on his own, this is what it had come down to.

The only thing that Zack had insisted upon was that she keep herself tucked down against the trunk of the wide tree that he'd chosen for them to make their move. She wasn't to look down the path behind them, so she didn't offer herself as a target for that rifle. Her weapon of choice, if things went wrong, was her stick-bat since she didn't want to bet her life, or his, on her ability to use the knife.

So here they were, her tucked against the base of the tree, partially hidden by thick bushes, and him, lying down across a branch about ten feet up with his knife at the ready, waiting.

And waiting.

Ten minutes passed, fifteen. At the twenty-minute mark, she risked a look up into the tree above her, only to see thick red drops of blood painting the side of the branch where Zack was lying, a reddish-brown stain spreading across the bark. It was the wound in his thigh, she realized. It must have started bleeding again. And the amount of blood that he'd lost was downright scary. She pulled herself to her feet, clutching her bat, while she stood on tiptoe looking up.

"Zack," she whispered, trying not to be too loud. "Zack?"

Nothing. His head was turned away from her. She couldn't tell if he was even conscious.

Dread curled in her stomach. She looked around then very carefully edged to the other side of the tree, trying to use the bushes at the base to stay as concealed as possible.

"Zack," she called, a little louder. His eyes were closed, she realized. Was he even breathing? Oh, no. What had she done by insisting on this plan? She shouldn't have second-guessed his first plan. She reached up with the stick and pushed on his left leg.

He groaned but didn't open his eyes. He shifted on the branch and suddenly pitched out of the tree. He landed, hard, on a group of bushes and then rolled out onto the ground, on his stomach, his head twisted to the side at an uncomfortable-looking angle.

Kaylee ran and sank to her knees beside him. His

eyes were still closed. She wanted to straighten his head but was afraid she'd hurt his neck.

"Zack," she whispered in his ear as she carefully felt for a pulse along his carotid. There, a steady beat beneath her fingertips. Thank God. "Zack?" she whispered again. Still nothing. She ran her hand along the back of his head, across his scalp. There, a golf ball–sized lump on the side of his head. Had he hit it against the branch while up in the tree? Is that why he was unconscious? She'd thought the bushes had broken his fall, kept his head from slamming against the ground. What if she was wrong? A fall from that high up, then hitting his head…he might never wake up from something like that.

Keep it together, she admonished herself. *You can't help him if you fall apart.*

She scrabbled back and checked his thigh, surprised to see that, no, it wasn't bleeding. Not much, anyway, certainly not enough to explain the amount of blood she'd seen on the tree branch. She ran her hands up and down both legs, his arms, then, desperate to find the source, she tried to roll him over. But he was too heavy. She leaned down to check his right side, shoving her hand beneath his body. It came out clean, no blood. She moved to his other side, and that was when she saw it.

An arrow, its evil-looking haft sticking out at an awkward angle, the point buried somewhere underneath him. Her breath left her in a rush. He'd been shot in the side, and his shirt was soaked in blood. But if he'd been shot, then that meant…she lunged for her makeshift bat just as footsteps sounded impossibly close.

"Drop it," a harsh voice ordered from directly behind her as her fingers wrapped around the wood. "Now."

Cold metal pressed against her temple. A gun.

She dropped the stick.

Handcuffs dangled in front of her face as he shook them out over her head.

"You know what to do, darlin'," he taunted.

A sob welled up in her throat as she took the cuffs and snapped them onto her wrists.

DIZZY. HOT, LIKE a sauna. Zack groaned and started to roll onto his side, but piercing, sharp pain stopped him. He forced his heavy eyelids open and stared in confusion at the ground, just inches from his face. How did he get here? He should have been… He jerked his head up and looked around. Kaylee, where was Kaylee?

He pressed his hands against the ground, hissing in a breath at the pain in his side, the throbbing in his head, the tug of the cut on his shoulder and the burning in his thigh. He was a wreck. But he didn't have time to worry about himself. If he was on the ground, instead of the tree branch where he'd planned to surprise their pursuer, and Kaylee wasn't around, something had gone horribly wrong.

"Kaylee?" he called out, unsurprised when she didn't answer. He cursed viciously. What had happened? He'd failed her, somehow. And where was she now? If that monster had her… He shook his head. Of course the monster had her, otherwise she'd be here, with him. More worried about him than herself. Too stubborn for her own good.

Ignoring the aches and pains in his body, he shoved to his knees. But the sharp tug on his left side couldn't be ignored. He glanced down, shocked when he saw the haft of an arrow, of all things. He looked up at the tree above him, the one he'd climbed. Their pursuer must have had a bow and shot him. His version of play, of having fun? Had he used the bow so Zack would die slowly, rather than kill him outright by using the rifle? There was no telling what had gone through the twisted man's mind. But Zack didn't remember being shot. The throbbing in his head was probably a good indicator of why.

He felt along the back and found the goose egg. Either he'd raised his head when he'd been shot with the arrow and slammed it against the branch directly above him, or he'd hit his head falling out of the tree. Either way, the memory of the event was gone.

He felt the skin around the haft and lifted his shirt. The business end of the arrow had gone completely through his side and protruded out from beside his navel. The wooden shaft formed a hard ridge. It appeared to have missed everything vital and had passed only through the outer layer of skin. For once, he'd gotten lucky. He hoped that streak held, because he'd need all the luck he could get to find and rescue Kaylee.

Gritting his teeth, he shoved himself to his feet and searched once again for the knife he'd been holding while up in the tree. There it was, at the base of the bush that was half-flattened from his fall. Two good things in a row. Maybe lady luck really was on his side.

Holding the arrow steady, he sawed through the shaft then grabbed the haft and yanked it out. It made a sickening, sucking sound and fresh blood welled up immediately. He pressed his hand against his side to staunch the bleeding while holding the knife in his other hand and eyeing the ground. There, footprints, and not his either. He tried to read what may have happened based on the way the two sets of prints slid at one point, stepped over each other at another spot.

And what he saw had him swearing all over again. The best he could tell, Kaylee had rushed over to him, the twin impressions of her knees clearly visible in the dirt. And then, the man who'd shot that arrow, the man who'd captured her and tortured her for months, had stepped behind her, surprising her. They'd left together, his shoeprints and her bare footprints going off in what appeared to be an easterly direction.

Eyeing the tree he'd been in earlier, he hurried over to it and started climbing.

A few minutes later he had an excellent view of a large portion of those two and a half million acres of swampland stretching out endlessly around him in every direction. He also saw something else—a road, a two-lane honest-to-goodness dirt and gravel road. It dead-ended about a half mile east at the beginning of a stretch of endless, golden saw grass that marked the beginning of a series of canals.

The road also extended for miles in the opposite direction. It had to lead to civilization eventually. Wait, what did he see way down the road? It had to be… He jerked back to the left as something came into his line of vision. He stiffened, watching with growing dread as a small pickup pulled out of the woods near that dead end and turned west on the road. It was too far away for him to make out faces, but he could pick Kaylee's petite, curvy form out anywhere. She was the passenger, and the driver was wearing a mask.

He jerked his head to the right, studying the many curves in the road, curves that wound around the marsh and canals and groups of cypress trees…curves that would force the truck to go slow to stay on the road. He made a mental calculation, picking a path through the woods that would act as a shortcut, hopefully placing him at one of those curves before the truck passed that way.

And then he was half sliding, half falling down the tree as fast as he could go. He jumped from the lowest branch, landing in one of the half-flattened bushes, flattening the rest of it. Then he was running once again, going as fast as he could in his odd-hitched gait, favoring his right thigh, arms and legs pumping.

THE SMALL TRUCK bumped and slid on the dirt and gravel road, forcing Kaylee's captor to drive much slower than he probably wanted to, especially around the sharp, deadly curves. She blinked to clear her vision, but it kept going double, probably because he'd slammed his pistol against the side of her head before tossing her into the passenger seat. He'd then looped the seat belt around the chain between her cuffs before securing it, effectively immobilizing her at an awkward angle with her hands trapped against the seat.

He'd wanted to do a lot more than that when he'd forced her to leave Zack lying unconscious on the path and had brought her to where he'd parked his truck just inside the woods. He'd already taken a few swipes at her with a knife before they'd gotten to the truck, leaving bloody gashes on her arms. His full collection of knives and chains had been lying in the back, along with his rifle and bow. But just as he'd bent down to lift her onto the tailgate, no doubt to make her lie down in the back so he could do his worst, the two-way radio in his cab had crackled to life.

Lieutenant Drew Shlafer's voice had rung out on some police frequency, letting the searchers know they'd found a damaged, abandoned white cargo van that matched the description given by witnesses at the rest stop. And that they had a lead on a pickup that had been stolen not far from where the van was found, leaving them to believe that if they located the pickup, they'd find Chief Scott and Miss Brighton. And then Drew had mentioned a particular area and the name of a road to be searched next. That was when her captor had stiffened and slammed the tailgate closed. He'd dragged her to the cab, where he'd taken out his frustration by coldcocking her on the side of the head with his pistol before shoving her inside.

After sliding into the driver's seat, he'd turned his eerie mask her way, his dark eyes flashing their hatred. "Don't think for one second that you're going to survive this. If I go down, so do you." He'd patted the pistol on his hip, so close and yet so impossible for her to grab with her hands trapped the way they were.

"The only reason I'm not killing you right now is because I may need a hostage." He'd leaned toward her. "And once I get out of here with my hostage, that's when your usefulness ends." He'd fingered her hair for a moment then flicked it. "I wanted more fun with you, more…quality time. Who knows, maybe it'll still work out and we'll get to spend many more pleasurable hours together, after all."

She had shivered with revulsion and he laughed.

Then he'd started the engine and the little truck took off down the gravel road. That had been ten minutes ago, and so far they hadn't seen anyone. No sign of any cops or searchers. No sirens. Maybe she'd misunderstood what the lieutenant had said, and her captor's reaction. Maybe the road he'd mentioned had nothing to do with this one.

She closed her eyes briefly, fighting the urge to cry, or just scream at the man whose sick, twisted desires had been inflicted on her and others. There was no humanity left in him, if indeed there had ever been. He didn't have a conscience or care in any way about the people whose lives he destroyed.

Like Zack's.

Her throat tightened with grief. Zack had suffered so much, all because he'd wanted to protect her. He was so noble, strong and yet so gentle with her. She'd never met anyone like him. It had been his quiet strength that had pulled her through those first agonizing, overwhelming days at the hospital. And every time since then, when she'd despaired of ever feeling normal or going through a single day without fear, it had been memories of his deep voice, his hand on her hand, that had bolstered her courage.

Please let him be okay. Please let him recover from his injuries and go on. He deserves to find someone to love, who'll love him just as fiercely as he once loved his fiancée, Jo Lynne.

Yes, he would be okay. She had to think that. The alternative was too devastating to contemplate.

The truck slowed again at the approach to another curve with a road sign showing a zigzag curve up ahead.

An object flew at the truck from the side of the road, flashing in the sunlight. *Boom!* The tire blew out. Beside her, the masked man swore and wrestled with the wheel as the truck skidded across the gravel, out of control. Kaylee had a quick glimpse of someone limping toward them from the cover of trees. Zack? Could it be? The truck twisted again, then its right wheels slipped over the edge of the road. Kaylee gasped and threw herself back against the seat as the pickup slammed into the side of a tree with a sickening crunch.

She shook her head to clear the buzzing sound in her ears, desperately trying to focus her bleary vision. Beside her, the masked man groaned, his chest slumped against the wheel. Somewhere in the back of her mind, Kaylee couldn't help a slight cheer. The man had used a seat belt as a rope to tie her but hadn't worn one himself. Sometimes karma was awesome.

He jerked back against the seat, looking out the window, eyes wide. He clawed for his pistol just as the driver's side door was thrown open. Hands reached in and hauled him out of the truck as he was raising the pistol.

Bam! Bam! Bam! Shots rang out and someone let

out a string of curses. Kaylee struggled against the seat belt, desperately trying to maneuver her body at an angle that would allow her to get some slack on her hands so she could unclick the seat belt.

Something cracked against the windshield and she bolted upright. A rock, gravel from the road, had flown up and now skittered across the hood and dropped to the ground. She lifted herself higher, trying to see what was happening. Zack, it was definitely Zack. He was on top of the masked man a few feet in front of the truck, pummeling him with both his fists, over and over and over. Her captor had given up fighting back and was whimpering and crying out like a wounded animal, throwing his hands up, desperately trying to block the blows.

Kaylee redoubled her efforts, twisting and tugging. *Click.* She finally got the seat belt to release but the chain was still stuck. She glanced over her shoulder at the road as she tugged and worked on the belt to unloop it from the cuffs. Her captor was no longer even trying to deflect the blows. His hands were down. His head whipped back and forth as Zack continued to slam his fists into him.

"Zack!" Kaylee yelled. But he didn't seem to hear her. "Zack, stop it! You're going to kill him!"

Still nothing. She didn't care if the masked man died. But she did care if he died like this, because it would forever be on Zack's conscience. She desperately yanked at the seat belt but it was hopelessly tied around the chain. Sirens sounded in the distance. She jerked her head up. Yes! The police must have been close by, after all. They'd heard the shots. But they'd be too late to stop Zack.

She threw herself back against the seat and lifted her legs, kicking them against the steering wheel. She managed one quick blare of the horn then slammed her foot down on it, over and over, honking at Zack and screaming his name, begging him to stop.

His head jerked up, and his right fist froze in mid-swing, ready to deal what surely had to be a death blow to the unconscious man lying beneath him. Like a savage animal, his entire body was coiled, ready to strike. With her fuzzy vision, she couldn't see the look in his eyes, but she imagined them filled with blood lust, an all-consuming rage and thirst for vengeance. She shook her head, quietly beseeching him to stop.

His shoulders finally slumped and he gave her a curt nod, lowered his fists. She sent up a silent prayer of thanks and smiled. He didn't return the smile. Instead, he turned around, bent over their captor's body. She tried to see what he was doing, but his back blocked her view. A moment later she could see him straighten and shake his head, before shoving himself to his feet.

The sirens were much louder now, and a four-wheel-drive sheriff's office truck came skidding around the far corner, lights flashing. It headed toward them, another truck following close behind.

Zack ignored them and strode to the pickup, to Kaylee. He tossed something inside on the dash—the leather mask, that was what he'd been doing, taking it off. And then he was cutting the seat belt. Without a word, he lifted her into his arms.

She put her hands around his neck, clinging to him as he carried her away from the truck. The first police vehicle stopped about twenty feet away. Drew Shlafer hopped out of the passenger side and ran toward them. The driver hopped out, as well, gun drawn as he hurried toward the body lying in the road.

Zack ignored both of them, just walked past Drew, whose mouth fell open at the sight of them, probably because Zack was covered in blood and limping, and Kaylee wasn't in much better shape herself.

"Hospital," Zack ordered as he stepped past the lieutenant. "She needs a doctor."

Drew immediately turned, barking orders to his men, with more arriving, sirens blaring. Then he ran to the truck and yanked the back door open just as Zack reached it. He lifted Kaylee inside, cradling her on his lap. Drew slammed the door, slid into the driver's seat and did a one-eighty, racing back down the road.

His eyes met Zack's in the mirror. "The masked man, he's—"

"Alive," Zack replied, his voice tight, clipped. "Only because Kaylee stopped me. I wanted to kill him."

She tightened her arms around him.

"His mask was gone," Drew said. "But I didn't get close enough to see him."

"Jasper Carraway," Zack said. "It was Jasper."

Drew shook his head. "No. It wasn't. They found the real Jasper Carraway's body in the panhandle. He was murdered several days ago, his body stashed in the woods behind his house." He reached over to the passenger seat as he steered around another curve then held up a picture for them to see in the back. "Is this the man you saw when you took off the mask?"

Kaylee lifted her head, trying to focus on the picture. It was just a fuzzy blur, and her head pounded from the effort. She closed her eyes and relaxed back against Zack.

"That's him," Zack confirmed. "That's the man who abducted Kaylee."

"And you," she whispered against his neck. "He abducted you, too."

He gently squeezed her in response.

"Hutch Mulcahy," Drew confirmed. "He must have killed the FFW officer and taken on his identity to insinuate himself into the search, to get close to Kaylee no doubt. You were right about the profile change. He'd been working at a landscaping company in Naples during the day. And he'd called in sick on the days of the abductions."

Zack's fingers gently stroked Kaylee's back as he continued to hold her tight. "Just get us to the hospital. Kaylee needs a doctor."

"You got it."

She lifted her head and stared at him in wonder. "You're the one who needs the doctor. You should let me go and let me check your injuries."

He cupped her face. "I'm never letting you go." And then he kissed her.

Epilogue

Kaylee stood in front of Mystic Glades's only church, waiting for her cue to go inside, while her new friends fussed over the short train of her wedding gown. Silver and Amber smiled at her as they arranged her veil, while Faye insisted on tying a small red-colored velvet bag to the garter on Kaylee's thigh.

"Trust me," she said, as she straightened, "that little bag is the secret to a hot, sex-filled honeymoon." Faye winked as Kaylee's face heated. "And there's always more where that came from. Stop in at my shop, The Moon and Star, anytime."

Silver rolled her eyes and gave a last pat to Kaylee's veil before she and Amber both stepped back. "When you and Zack return from your trip to Kentucky, of all places, you should stay in the bridal suite at my bed-and-breakfast." She waved toward the building that was a short distance away from the little clapboard church.

"Or better yet," Amber added, "come stay with me

and Dex in the condo we just bought in New York. We'll take you for a carriage ride in Central Park."

Kaylee smiled through threatening tears at these three women, all of whom had found their own heroes in Mystic Glades, just like she had. She aimed a particularly warm smile at Silver, who was Cole's wife, and who had helped prepare her for the ups and downs of being a law-enforcement officer's wife, since Silver and Cole had married not long ago themselves.

"Thank you all," she said. "You were so nice to my parents." She waved toward the church, knowing her mother sat in the front pew, and that her father stood just inside the double doors, ready to walk her down the aisle. "And you've welcomed me to this town, and into your hearts. I couldn't ask for more supportive friends."

They all hugged and then her cue—the "Wedding March"—started up inside.

"This is it," Faye said, reaching for one of the door handles while Amber reached for the other. "Ready?"

Was she ready? It had been six months since Zack had saved her from the masked man, limping and bleeding and pushing himself to the limit to find a shortcut through the woods to stop the truck at one of the curves. And then he'd thrown the only weapon he had, the knife, blowing out the tire and then facing Kaylee's abductor with nothing but his bare hands. The man was amazing and had risked everything—

for her. Now her former captor was in prison, where he'd never hurt anyone else, ever again. Because of Zack.

She'd been so desperately in love with him that she hadn't wanted to wait longer than it took for both of them to be released from the hospital before starting a life together. But he'd insisted on her taking the time to recover, in mind and spirit, not just body, before making a decision like that. And he wanted her to wait through the trial, saying she needed to focus on that before adding anything else to her plate. And he'd been right. She'd needed that time more than she'd realized.

She'd finally opened up to her therapist and was working through her fears. Surprisingly, testifying in court had been an important part of that therapy. Finally seeing the face of the man whom she'd thought of as the devil, as all-powerful, had made her see him for what he really was. Just a man. He no longer had the power to hurt her.

Of course she'd also had to tell her parents the full story, prior to the trial, so they wouldn't be surprised to hear it from the media. That had been one of the hardest things she'd ever done. Especially because she'd misjudged them so badly. By trying to protect them, she'd hurt them. And she'd vowed never to lie to them again.

Yes, Zack had been right. She'd had a lot to work through. But she'd come a long way. Were there still some dark times? Nights when she woke herself screaming? Yes, but they were further and further apart now. And she had no doubt that one day the nightmares would disappear forever.

She was happy—really happy—for the first time in a long time. She was marrying the love of her life, Zack Scott. And then he was taking her back to his hometown, to Murray, Kentucky, to spend some time with his very large extended family, many of whom were sitting inside the church right now.

Just like Amber, Silver, Faye and other Mystic Glades residents had welcomed her, so had Zack's family. She'd been so worried when she'd met his three brothers, his mom, his dad, because she knew they must have all loved Zack's first fiancée, Jo Lynne, very much. But there was plenty of room in their hearts for Kaylee, too. His mama told Kaylee she held an extra special place in her heart, because Kaylee had brought Zack out of mourning and back into the light. By taking Zack into her heart, Kaylee had given his mother back her son.

The doors swung open and were propped back. Then, one by one, her three matrons of honor—Amber, Silver and Faye—headed down the aisle. And then it was her turn. She kissed her father's cheek and put her arm through the crook of his elbow. Then he slowly walked her down the red carpet.

Kaylee smiled through her happy tears at the overflowing pews on either side of the aisle. It seemed like the whole town had turned out for the wedding, people she was still getting to know, like Buddy Johnson, who seemed to own half of Mystic Glades. She blinked in surprise to see another man, leaning against the wall with a snake wrapped around his neck. The man grinned and waved then resumed petting the snake as if it was a dog.

She smiled back, wondering what other types of surprises she had in store living in a place like this. It was quirky and strange and absolutely perfect so far. Because Zack was here, which was all she needed to make her life complete.

He watched her from the front of the church, his broad shoulders encased in a gorgeous, black suit. Surely, there'd never been a finer looking groom. Even his three handsome brothers, who stood with Faye, Amber, and Silver, couldn't compete with how extraordinary Zack looked. Then again, she supposed she was biased.

As she neared the front of the church, she shivered with delight at the way Zack's deep blue eyes seemed to devour her. Impatient now, she urged her father to hurry, probably a little too fast, judging by the surprised smile that spread across Zack's face.

Before her father could give her away or the preacher could say a single word, she raised the edge of her veil and planted a searing kiss against her husband-to-be's mouth.

He eagerly deepened the kiss, much to the amusement of his brothers, who whistled their approval. While most of the church dissolved into laughter, her new friend Faye urged them on with a loudly whispered, "You go, girl."

The sounds of both the preacher and her father loudly clearing their throats had her reluctantly ending the kiss and stepping back. Her grinning groom gave her a sexy wink that nearly brought her to her knees.

An eternity later, after her father officially gave her away and sat beside her beaming mother, she smiled up at Zack. "I love you."

"Not half as much as I love you," he assured her. "Now let's do this thing so I can take you somewhere private." He winked again and helped her arrange her veil over her face for the ceremony.

She took his arm and faced a future filled with hope and security, and best of all, the warm light of her husband's love to keep the dark shadows at bay. Oh, she knew there would still be times when the horrors of her past would haunt her. But she also knew that she never had to face her fears alone again. She would always have this wonderful man beside her, for better or worse.

Just when she'd decided the preacher was never going to finish, he pronounced them husband and wife. This time it was Zack who lifted her veil. The look on his face was almost reverent. He stared down at her as if he thought he was the luckiest person alive to have her. But of course that wasn't true. She was the luckiest one, to have him.

The preacher told Zack he could kiss his bride.

And so he did, quite thoroughly.

* * * * *

COMING NEXT MONTH FROM

H HARLEQUIN®

INTRIGUE

Available September 20, 2016

#1665 STILL WATERS
Faces of Evil • by Debra Webb
With her prints on the murder weapon, Amber Roberts is the primary person of interest in the murder of a man she hardly knew. Is she a killer or the next victim?

#1666 NAVY SEAL TO DIE FOR
SEAL of My Own • by Elle James
After witnessing multiple attempts to kill sexy Stealth Operations Specialist Becca Smith, navy SEAL Quentin Lovett offers to cover her six while she follows leads to find her father's killer.

#1667 ARMY RANGER REDEMPTION
Target: Timberline • by Carol Ericson
Scarlett Easton has always shied away from the kidnappings cases that haunted her reservation twenty years ago, but as a new threat entangles her with army ranger Jim Kennedy, they both must face the darkness in their pasts.

#1668 KENTUCKY CONFIDENTIAL
Campbell Cove Academy • by Paula Graves
When Captain Connor McGinnis discovers his dead wife is very much alive, pregnant and in grave danger, he puts his life on the line to protect her and save their marriage.

#1669 COWBOY CAVALRY
The Brothers of Hastings Ridge Ranch • by Alice Sharpe
Can Frankie Hastings and Kate West set aside the long-buried secrets of their pasts in order to stay ahead of the devious mastermind bent on destroying their future?

#1670 DUST UP WITH THE DETECTIVE
by Danica Winters
Deputy Blake West never dreamed she'd reunite with her childhood friend Jeremy Lawrence in investigating the circumstances of his brother's death, and as they begin to uncover the truth, danger might be much closer than they suspect.

YOU CAN FIND MORE INFORMATION ON UPCOMING HARLEQUIN® TITLES, FREE EXCERPTS AND MORE AT WWW.HARLEQUIN.COM.

HICNM0916

REQUEST YOUR FREE BOOKS!
2 FREE NOVELS PLUS 2 FREE GIFTS!

⊕HARLEQUIN®

INTRIGUE

BREATHTAKING ROMANTIC SUSPENSE

HI15

SPECIAL EXCERPT FROM

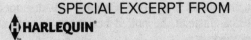
H HARLEQUIN®
™

INTRIGUE

After witnessing multiple attempts to kill sexy
Stealth Operations Specialist Becca Smith,
Navy SEAL Quentin Lovett offers to cover her
six while she tracks down her father's killer.

Read on for a sneak preview of
A NAVY SEAL TO DIE FOR,
the third book in Elle James's thrilling quartet
A SEAL OF MY OWN.

The door at the end of the train car opened and a man
stepped through. Becca's pulse leaped. She reached out
and gripped Quentin's leg. "Speak of the devil. He's
headed this way. We need to hide. Right now." She shrank
against Quentin's side, trying to get out of sight of the
man heading directly toward them.

"Kiss me," Quentin urged.

"What?" She shot a glance at him. She'd wanted to
kiss him all day long and wondered if he'd ever try to kiss
her again. "Now?"

"Yes, now. Hurry." He swept the cap off her head,
ruffled her hair, finger-combing it to let it fall around
her shoulders in long, wavy curls. Then he gripped her
arms and pulled her against him, pressing his lips to hers.
Using her hair as a curtain to hide both of their faces,
Quentin prolonged the kiss until Ivan passed them and
walked through to the next car.

When the threat was gone, Quentin still did not let go of Becca. Instead, he pulled her across his lap and deepened the kiss.

Becca wrapped her arms around his neck. If Ivan came back that way, she never knew. All she knew was that if she died that moment, she'd die a happy woman. Quentin's kiss was that good.

The train lurched, throwing them out of the hold they had on each other. Becca lifted her head and stared around the interior of the train car. For the length of that soul-defining kiss, she'd forgotten about Ivan and the threat of starting a gunfight on a train full of people. Heat surged through her and settled low in her belly, and a profound ache radiated inside her chest. She wanted to kiss Quentin and keep kissing him. More than that, she wanted to make love to him and wake up beside him every day.

But she realized how impossible that would be. They were two very different people who worked in highly dangerous jobs, based out of different parts of the country. Nothing about a relationship with Quentin would work. She had to remind herself that he was a ladies' man—a navy guy with a female conquest in every port.

Don't miss A NAVY SEAL TO DIE FOR,
available October 2016 wherever
Harlequin® Intrigue books and ebooks are sold.

www.Harlequin.com

HIEXP0916

Love the Harlequin book you just read?

Your opinion matters.

Review this book on your favorite book site, review site, blog or your own social media properties and share your opinion with other readers!

Be sure to connect with us at:
Harlequin.com/Newsletters
Facebook.com/HarlequinBooks
Twitter.com/HarlequinBooks

THE WORLD IS BETTER WITH
Romance

Harlequin has everything from contemporary, passionate and heartwarming to suspenseful and inspirational stories.

Whatever your mood, we have a romance just for you!

Connect with us to find your next great read, special offers and more.

f /HarlequinBooks

🐦 @HarlequinBooks

www.HarlequinBlog.com

www.Harlequin.com/Newsletters

⟨H⟩ HARLEQUIN®

A *Romance* FOR EVERY MOOD™

www.Harlequin.com